Naked Erotica

I sat in the stern and closed my eyes, enjoying the lift and lap of the oars in the water, the pleasant surge and dip of the boat under his powerful stroking. I thought of his fingers on my back. I thought of him, naked. Me naked, with him. I slit my eyes. Imagined straddling him on that seat and pressing myself open right over him. His cock, engorging, would rise straight up into me.

He said, "Do you realize you're moving back and forth with me?"

"Force of habit," I said. Laughing, blushing. "Stroke. Stroke. Now, faster."

Naked Erotica
26 Sultry Stories of Skin on Skin

edited by Alison Tyler
foreword by Barbara Pizio,
executive editor,
Penthouse Variations

Naked Erotica
Copyright 2004 by Pretty Things Press
all stories copyright 2004 by the respective authors
All Rights Reserved
Cover Design: Eliza Castle

First Pretty Things Press Edition 2004

First Printing 2004

ISBN: 1-57612-197-6

Manufactured in the United States of America
Published by Pretty Things Press
www.prettythingspress.com

987654321

For SAM.

"It's not true I had nothing on. I had the radio on."
—Marilyn Monroe.

Foreword

The feel of skin on skin is the perfect embodiment of naked lust: The passionate whisper of flesh gliding against flesh. The satisfying tangle of limbs and desires. Getting lost in that timeless moment of discovery, where the world disappears and there is nothing but the seemingly endless landscape of heat and flesh. Each curve and slope uncovers a new emotion and sensation, fanning the flames of lust.

Tenille Brown's "The Art of Exposure" shows us that sometimes the chance occurrence of an illicit glimpse of bare skin can take you from a teasing moment to a passionate affair. Or it might be the briefest of electric touches, as in Cate Robertson's "Stroking"—fingers brushing over a patch of flesh and that single moment that sparks an unquenchable ardor.

Throughout this book you'll experience the thrilling anticipation of a lover's body being revealed. While the first time has its own special frisson, the excitement never really fades, as M. Christian so beautifully describes in "Jess Undressed." A number of stories in this collection revel in the newfound joy of such carnal discovery, as well as the inherent beauty of the nude body. Rachel Kramer Bussel's "Touch" is a heartfelt journey, describing the ecstatic wonder that can be found in a lover stripped bare, and how that profound beauty amazes her awestruck partner.

Other tales presented here branch out and explore what it really means to be naked in every delicious sense. Naked is more than simply not wearing clothes. That is just the beginning. In Savanna Stephen Smith's "Naked Ambition" the narrator describes her lust for power and reveals her amorous journey to the top of the corporate ladder. Tulsa Brown's "Radiance," however, demonstrates the reverse, revealing how empowering passion can be. An older businesswoman helps a younger one blossom into a self-assured woman in one simple, sexy evening. Stripping your inhibitions, along with your clothes, creates a whole new world where desire can conquer all.

Having the courage to lay bare all of one's fantasies is perhaps the bravest act of them all. Alex M. Quinlin's "Bare to the Waist" tells the story of a couple who shows us the power of revealing their longing for dominance and submission. This shameless offering of themselves and their private dreams leads them to a more intensely fulfilling love life. Saskia Walker's "Skin on Skin" is another tale of transformation. Her piece introduces us to a woman, dressed in her best fetish wear, who engages in the flirtatious ritual of the club scene. She later sheds her outer skin as she joins a group of passionate revelers at a very special private party, helping her realize her heart's desire.

All of these stories explore the many facets of naked lust, laying bare their wonderful possibilities. Their characters have nothing to hide. Join them on their journey, as they fulfill their secret fantasies. You may very well find yourself wanting to get naked, too!

Introduction

I remember the first time I was naked with a boy.

Totally, completely, *utterly* naked.

I was eighteen, away at college and crushing hard on a junior named Nick, an intellectual Elvis Costello-type who was three years older than me and educated in a variety of ways that had nothing to do with his major. All of the girls on our dorm floor were crazy for him, but he didn't seem to notice any of us. That is, not until he saw me wearing a pair of plaid pajamas while I lay sprawled out on my skinny twin bed studying. As soon as my roommate left us to ourselves in the tiny space, he sat on the edge of the mattress, twined his fingers with mine and whispered, "I like your pjs."

"Yeah?" I asked, surprised. They were old and faded, blue-and-green plaid like a boy's.

"They look great on you," he insisted, "but they'd look even better on the floor."

To me, this statement was the height of seduction. He liked my pjs. He'd like them even more *off* me. That meant he wanted to see me naked. And I'd never been naked—not *all the way* naked—with a boy before.

I sat up and worked the buttons slowly. Not out of any strip-tease effort, but because I was so shy. Nick watched, obviously spellbound, and as I felt his gray-green eyes on me, I discovered the thrill in becoming undressed. The action of taking off my clothes was almost as exciting as what happened after I got those clothes off. (I say "almost.")

Since that night, I've learned all about the pleasures of nakedness. Nude, bare, stripped down. I know it all. I know that sometimes you can feel more naked when you leave on one little item: a thong to be pushed aside, a velvet glove to stroke up and down your lover's back. Even a choker, or a collar, can make you feel extra exposed while being almost entirely naked. And I know that when a lover undresses you, *that* can be the most exceptional type of nakedness.

The authors in this collection have ingeniously explored the concept of stripped-down stories, conjuring up some of the most revealing tales I've had the pleasure to read. Several of these creative writers focused on the items of clothing that get in the way of being naked, while others wrote about the most naked part of an undressed lover. (Check out Maxim Jakubowski's "Utterly Nude.") "The Story Her Body Told" is from the point-of-view of a hot-blooded, lustful masseur whose fantasy ultimately comes true, while "Nude Dreams or Naked Reality?" focuses on an erotic nightmare most of us can relate to personally. Read "Lucy Laid Bare" to delve further into the concept of exposing something previously hidden, and "Radiance" to revel in the ultimate glory of a naked woman's body.

I could continue, exposing this book in a sexy little strip-tease, taunting you with tidbits from each and every story in the collection. But now it's time to follow a bit of advice from Tommy Lee. As he suggests, "Get Naked," curl up in your favorite cozy chair, and prepare to be warmed by the heat in these explosively erotic stories. But before you do, let me tell you a little secret: *I'm* naked right now...

Your editor, laid bare,
Alison Tyler

JESS UNDRESSED
by M. Christian

Smiling, Jess got up.

Manx stayed on the futon, sprawled on his side. It was a "way too damned early in the—" kind of morning. You know the type: sunlight screaming through bare windows, sleep like bricks on eyelids, alarm like all the demons of hell screaming in pain. *That* kind of morning.

Manx lay like the wounded.

"Come on, baby," Jess said, leaning over him to turn off the alarm.

Manx made a noise somewhere between a grunt and a word.

"New day dawning," Jess said, standing, stretching elastically.

Manx grumbled and rolled over, blinking sticky sleep out of his eyes, this time a word—definitely—on his lips.

Jess: Standing next to their bed, barefoot, bare-assed. She was a small girl—she had to stand on her tip-toes and reach way above her head to make six feet—but she was a perfect miniature. Without reference, say Manx's six-three, she could have been any size, look anyone in the eyes.

She was lean and trim, all muscle and smooth, fine skin. Starting at where his eyes first landed, Manx saw her feet (as if for the first time): tiny toes painted navy blue. Baby toes, on dancer's feet. "Finely turned ankles" (and for the first time he knew what that meant) leading up to strong, strong calves that made, when you added in her perfectly formed thighs, beautiful legs. Legs, Manx realized, looking at Jess's, were something that are very hard to describe but, damn, you knew a good pair when you saw them and, damn, Jess had mighty fine legs.

Still moving, still stretching, he watched as the perfect moon of her ass turned with her exercises. Jess had a happy and pert ass, a lean and tight one—almost like a girl's and not like a woman's. Her skin was white but not pale, more like marble than like milk, and her crease was delightfully pale pink.

The small of her back was a gentle slope from the parade of her spine to the hard rise of her ass. Her curve was almost a perfect one, like her legs—hard to pin down, but obvious to the eye, especially to Manx's eyes.

"Do you want to stay in bed all day?"

"Maybe, maybe—" Manx said, stretching out his own body, hearing his bones creak and pop and feeling his face tingle then flex with his first yawn of the day—then Jess turned and Manx lost whatever he was going to say.

In one quick, supple/fluid move, Jess twisted around, showing Manx her sweet little rounded belly, her innie navel, and the sparse ginger forest between her legs. Sparse, yes, but just enough so that Manx had a delicious view of her plush mons and wide cleft. Then, to add the perfect topping to the sweet, sweet view, Jess turned and touched her toes— zapping Manx completely, utterly dumb at the sight of that girlie ass parting with her elegant movement to show the fat lips (more pink, lots more pink) of her puss.

Then she straightened, planted her butterfly quick hands on her hips and gazed back over her straight and strong shoulders to fix Manx with an immobilizing smile. She turned again, smiling all the while, to give Manx a better view.

Ah, thought Manx looking at Jess's breasts. Ah: not really a word, more like a feeling, like a kind of quiet had dropped over his mind at the sight of Jess's breasts. He was never one to admit it, almost not to himself, but he was a tit man. He liked their weight, their heavy silkiness, their beautiful shapes (all of them), and their lovely nipples. Even their name sounded sweet and playful: tits. Jess certainly had playful tits, and, god knew, Manx liked to play with them.

Jess's breasts were pointed, like sweeping gestures of skin. Soft as to be almost (but only almost) not there when Manx touched them. When Jess turned sideways, they would peak out three fingers, maybe four, beyond her arms. On her, on her slight body, they looked big but in Manx's hands they were small and oh-so-just right.

Jess was smiling, very, very wide. "Are you getting up, or what?"

But it was Jess's face that did it, really did it: she was an elf, a sprite, a nymph. One look at her and people smiled. She had that power, those planes of cheeks, nose, forehead, and lips (tasty). Her face was capped by a mad torrent of red curls that stopped just short of splashing down on her shoulders. Jess was small and lithe, and her face was perfect for her: a laughing butterfly, a joyful faery. Her eyes smiled, too, with her cheeks and lips, and flashed green mischief.

Her body made Manx's body warm, but Jess's face made him hot.

"I'm up, I'm up ... or at least parts of me are," Manx said, cupping his cock, feeling the heat—relishing in the pressure surge that rolled from deep inside.

"Well, I guess there's just no getting you out of bed today, is there?" Jess said, sitting down on the futon next to Manx and planting a quick, dry kiss on his lips.

"I bet, though, that there's a damned good chance of me getting you back into bed," Manx said, throwing the heavy sheets aside to give Jess a good view of himself and what he was doing.

Jess had gotten up, but seeing Manx she smiled—then went down.

RADIANCE
by Tulsa Brown

"But, Lise, you promised you'd go to the Christmas party with me."

"Darrel, that was before we broke up," I said.

"I told everyone a month ago you'd be coming."

"You should have found another date."

"I haven't been well." Darrel sniffled. "Besides, you know I miss you." His voice tugged on me, a dog pawing my leg under the table.

I sighed. "I'll see if I can find a dress."

Darrel Groening was lank-haired and lean, forever on the verge of a cold. I'd met him the previous spring and within fifteen minutes I'd known he wasn't the right species, never mind the right person. Yet I'd limped through a whole excruciating summer with him, and taken two more months to break it off. That was because I'd been born in Trent, Minnesota, where women had five more commandments than everyone else:

1. Never accept a compliment
2. Never refuse a gracious invitation.
3. Never pay full price.
4. Never complain.
5. Never break your word.

They weren't written down anywhere, but growing up I'd heard them more often than the other ten. When I'd moved to New York at the age of twenty-five, I didn't have to pack them—they were already under my skin.

Despite his precarious health, Darrel was pretty sharp. He not only figured out the extra commandments, he learned to play them like a video game. Extending number 2 into number 5 was a particular skill of his. And sex? Well, he was lucky there was number 4.

The inevitable party came too soon. I found myself in the corporate ballroom of a Manhattan office building one night in mid-December, against my will and entirely with my consent. Darrel put on a brave front for a man with terminal sinus congestion, and he wheeled me around the room on his arm, showing me off like a new watch. I was alarmed to discover how much people already knew about me, but even more irritated by his introduction.

"This is my girlfriend, Lise. It rhymes with 'please.'"

I smiled through gritted teeth.

"My, she is a little thing," big, beautiful people boomed at me. The term in Trent, Minnesota is "slight," as in "slight women shouldn't wear loud colors," and "slight women should never look too happy—it makes all the other women miserable."

There was no danger of that. I was lost in the swirl of glamorous strangers, wearing a simple satin dress in pastel blue with dyed-to-match sandals, a direct consequence of commandment number 3. Surrounded by chic cocktail black, I felt like an escaped bridesmaid. I downed two glasses of wine and wondered how I could feign illness without igniting Darrel's competitive streak.

"Ooh, boy, watch out for this one," he whispered abruptly in my ear. "Major corporate bitch at three o'clock."

Even from halfway across the room, I decided Maybird Howe was the most extraordinary-looking woman I'd ever seen. A tall, generously proportioned African American, she broke enough rules of propriety to make the women of Trent howl. Full breasts swelled dangerously over her low cut gown, and her bare arms were nearly as large as my thighs—and certainly more curvaceous. She walked toward us in a slow, swaying undulation, her gold and red beaded dress shimmering. She looked like Mardi Gras at night, a rave of color against her dark, abundant flesh.

I was mesmerized at first, too intimidated to speak. Maybird seemed to float on a smooth cloud of confidence, and even her small talk sparkled with wit. When she looked at me, I felt I was standing in a sunbeam. Where did a woman come from, I wondered, to have this kind of radiance?

Darrel ducked away shortly after the introductions, supposedly to get me another drink. Maybird showed no sign of leaving, although I was sure I was boring her to blindness. I struggled to find the voice I knew I used to have.

"Is Maybird really your name?" I asked finally.

She arched an eyebrow and tilted her head. "Is that limp noodle really your fiancee?"

"No! Oh, God, no." Is that what he'd been telling people? I fluttered and flapped like an alarmed bird, desperate that she know the truth. A slow smile lit up her round, calm face.

"I'm glad. His office is only on the fifteenth floor, you know. A splendid creature like you should be dating well above the twentieth."

The words made me hum with warm, unexpected pleasure, but she'd nailed me directly on number 1. I backed away from the compliment so fast I could have knocked someone over.

Maybird watched me, still smiling, yet there was a new intensity to her liquid, lioness eyes.

"Come up to my office. I want my view to enjoy you," she said.

Her view to enjoy me? Was I drunk or was she teasing me? Yet I did want to go with her, more than I'd wanted anything in a long time.

"Well, maybe for a few minutes," I said.

Riding the elevator up to the thirty-seventh floor, I was engulfed by Maybird's presence, the dizzying scent of her perfume, chrysanthemums or another lush, heavy flower. I found myself gazing at her gown, wondering what her generous hip would feel like if I ran my hand over it, the soft press of flesh under the sleek, nubbly surface of the beadwork. I was shocked that I wasn't shocked.

She had magnetic key cards for everything—the elevator, the closed hallway, her own office. Leading me through this last door, she switched on two wall sconces, but the rich oak paneling and leather furniture were already softly illuminated. All of Manhattan was lighting up this room.

"Oh," I breathed. The window was the length of one wall, a magnificent, glittering panorama. It drew me over without a thought and I stood, hands on the waist-high sill, steadying myself against the thrilling rush of vertigo.

"Now do you see why you should date above the twentieth floor?" Maybird asked. "Beauty deserves beauty."

I turned with a self-conscious laugh, prepared to argue, but the nervous noise died in my throat. She was very close now, and I was silenced by the sienna landscape in front of me, the near-nakedness of her bare arms and plunging cleavage. Maybird leaned her generous ass against the edge of the desk, beadwork rubbing the wood in an exciting crystalline growl.

She smiled. "Take your shoes off, little miss, if they hurt your feet."

The name nipped me, a tiny bite in a secret place. Yet, she was right—I was sliding forward in my cheap sandals, toes cramping. I stepped out of them with relief, dropping three inches in front of her.

"And your stockings."

"Pardon?"

"When you stand on my desk, I don't want you to slip."

Had I heard right? I was bewildered. I glanced out the plate glass window again, at the vast spread of buildings glowing in the December night. I could see right into the lighted offices across the street, the abandoned desks and filing cabinets clearly defined in the hard fluorescence. And if I could see them...

Maybird moved in closer and stroked my hair, easing it off my neck. She left her warm hand on my bare shoulder, and the heat permeated through my whole body.

"They've all gone home. And if someone did see, do you think they'd recognize you tomorrow on the sidewalk? You're safe, you're free." Her smile was superior, glimmering with seasons of experience. "I want my view to enjoy you, little miss."

That name again. My sex lips were thickening between my thighs. I felt a long way from Trent, emboldened by two glasses of wine and the touch of this strong, exciting woman. How old was she? Thirty-five? Forty? All I knew was that her voice held me in thrall. I wanted to fall into it, like a river, and be carried away. I turned discreetly and reached under my skirt to slide the pantyhose off. For a brazen second I thought of slipping out of my panties, too, but...no.

My bare legs whispered in surprise against each other. Maybird held out her hand for the soft wad of my stockings, which she tossed into the wastepaper basket. I stared after them, stung by a parting shot of conscience. They'd cost fifteen dollars.

"Up you go."

I stepped onto the leather chair, then up to the gleaming wooden desk top, straightening slowly, lightheaded with the sudden height and strange perspective. It didn't seem like the same room anymore. I was facing the office's back wall as Maybird's voice drifted out to me.

"Turn around to the window. Tell me what you see."

I swivelled with tiny, cautious steps, bare feet sticking to the polished surface. Then I laughed, exhilarated.

"Oh, my God, it's beautiful! It's like the Milky Way." From this new angle, the hard edge of the sill vanished from my field of vision. All I could see were endless lights, a galaxy glittering on and on. If I stared forward, there was no office and no window, and my perception of depth dissolved. I was simply floating in the lights, as one of them. It was magical, and strangely... familiar. For an instant I was a child again, lying under the vast prairie night sky, believing I was one of the stars.

"Yes, the Milky Way," Maybird murmured. Then, "Take your dress off. Let it fall to your feet."

My clit swelled at the unthinkable wickedness. To bare my body in front of a full length window, simply for another woman's pleasure, so that she could...what?

Enjoy the view.

"*Now*, little miss."

The demand in her voice was thrilling. My heart fluttered as I reached behind and grasped the tab, the zipper teeth parting in a purr of acquiescence. My pussy was slick, the engorged lips pressing against the taut crotch of my cotton panties. I wondered what color I'd chosen this morning, and if it would suit her.

A rustle told me Maybird was still waiting. I shrugged off the tiny straps and let the fabric fall into a tumble of blue satin around my ankles.

"Ahh." Her sigh was a croon of appreciation, a caress along my naked back. The sound spoke to my nipples, which finished hardening in the open air, aching to be touched. A tiny corner of my mind was aghast, unable to believe I was truly standing here, exposed to the night city. Yet the rest of me wasn't thinking at all. I was simply part of the sky, a wet and throbbing star, beautiful, powerful, ravenous.

The swish of her gown pulled me back to earth. I didn't dare look down as her breath swept over the back of my legs, but when she opened her mouth in a luscious kiss on my calf, a hot V of pleasure shot up through me. I swayed.

"I might fall," I whispered.

"All right, sit down."

I lowered myself to the desktop, letting her pull my dress away so it wouldn't be crushed. She shook out the wrinkles and crossed the room to drape it carefully over a chair. I sat on the desk with my legs dangling, a child who'd been perched on the counter to stay out of the way. I desperately wanted to touch myself and didn't dare.

Maybird sauntered back to me, her holiday gown swinging with its own luxurious weight, her brown eyes gleaming in a tease. A laughing lioness. As she drew up against the desk, I spread my knees wide to encompass her ample hips, and reached up to embrace her. She caught my wrists and firmly returned my hands to my sides, palms flat on the desk.

"I have a ruler in my drawer," she said pleasantly. "Don't make me get it out."

My clit throbbed at the startling thought.

Maybird kissed me, a sweet sucking of astonishing power. I felt as if she were drawing my sex up into her mouth. She cupped my breasts, rolling my hard nipples into tight points. I spread my legs painfully as I tried to inch closer to her curving belly, a vain hope of rubbing my pussy against her beaded dress. I moaned with mindless want, a hungry little animal.

At last, she stroked me between the legs with her thumb, a stripe of pleasure that made me gasp.

"My, those panties are nice and wet, little miss."

"Oh, yes...oh, please." I tried not to whimper.

"Lie down on my desk."

I stretched out on the spacious wooden surface, and it was as hard and uncomfortable as I feared—for half a minute. After that I forgot about it completely. Maybird unzipped her own gown and eased her huge, soft breasts from their confinement, bending over to gather me into an earthy embrace. I suckled on one and stroked the other, nursing eagerly on the plump, heavy flesh. She stripped my panties off and pushed my knees to my chest, my pussy a wet crescent that she opened, stroked and teased.

Finally she plunged two fingers deep into my cunt, her thumb still lodged against my erect clit. For a fleeting second I thought of how it must look through her window, the pale shock of my slender schoolgirl's body curled up in her dark arms, nursing on her like a child, getting fucked by her strong hand. But I was beyond caring. I wasn't of this earth, my planet was pleasure, rocking, sucking, moaning.

Coming. My inner muscles clutched, spasms of bliss shaking me in pulsing white waves. I ground and twisted against her hand, thrusting my orgasm over one crest, then another, riding it greedily, joy bursting in my tits and toes. And all the while I was enveloped by the softest pillow in the world.

It was so strange to get dressed again. The concept of clothes and a life outside this room seemed alien to me. I glanced in the wastebasket at my stockings, and it was hard to remember what they were for, never mind that I'd sighed over their loss.

I noticed Maybird watching me, her eyes occasionally glancing at the desktop, the place where I'd shed myself and become one of the stars. I was haunted by the mystery. What had she seen in me, or heard in my voice? How had she known what the view would do to me? What she would do to me?

"Where are you from?" I asked.

Maybird's face was as calm and luminous as polished oak, but there was a glimmer in her eyes. "Oh, nowhere, really. Just a small city in the mid-west."

I felt a clutch. "Not...Trent."

The game was up and she smiled broadly. "No, I'm from Arthur, Minnesota. But it's very close, hardly a day's run—"

"—for a lame dog," I finished the colloquialism for her, stunned. The revelation opened up inside me. No wonder Maybird had my number. She had them all, 1 through 5— the damning extra commandments we'd both grown up with. And yet here she was in front of me, sensual, self-assured, beaming beauty and quiet power. Radiance. It gave me a shot of hope that bubbled out in a laugh.

"You know, I don't think I'm going to say goodbye to my 'fiancee' on the way out," I said.

"No, I don't think you are." Maybird extended her hand and I took it, and we stepped into the polished hallway, two celestial bodies glowing in a new night.

STROKING
by Cate Robertson

I was serving bar in the clubhouse when he came in with Don and the team. I noticed him right away, but not for his rower's physique: rowing clubs are full of broad shoulders, deep chests, and long, well-muscled arms. He caught my eye for two reasons: one, his hair was collar-length and astonishingly silver. Two, beneath his relaxed exterior lurked something fierce and dark, an animal intensity.

Don said, "Clare, a round of cold ones when you're ready."

The August night was so sultry that everyone had crowded onto the deck. As I carried out a tray filled with sweating glasses into the festive glow of patio lights, I met the glitter of his blue eyes. A day's growth of stubble on his angular jaw. Older than me, fortyish? He was lounging with an ankle crossed over his knee, his thigh muscles straining against his khakis. When he smiled at me, his mouth curved up suggestively at the corner.

Don did the introductions.

"Clare, this is Jack Rettigan. Old coaching buddy of mine from Vancouver. Jack, Clare Malley. My best cox."

"Hello, darling," he said. We clasped hands. A rower's palm, dry, firmly callused.

"I guess you're here for Regatta Week. Are you competing?" I said.

He nodded." It's my first time this far east. I've got a junior ladies' team, and Don's got us rowing, too, in the masters." His voice was rough-edged, warm as an embrace.

Don said, "Jack's coaching in the national program in September. You might get recruited." He winked at me.

Jack said, "Don tells me you're a superb coxswain."

I said, "He would say that. He trained me."

Jack chuckled.

Don said, "False modesty. Clare knows rowing inside out. She just didn't grow big enough to scull competitively."

Jack said, "Come closer, darling. Let me see you."

He drew me to him, his arm muscles taut around my hips. The strength of rowers is contained, explosive. His hand traveled over me with the practiced intimacy typical of those old-fashioned coaches who assess athletic condition by touch.

He clasped my forearm, stroked it. Squeezed my biceps, then my thigh. His thumb and fingers were knowing, expert.

He said, "What are you, five four? One-twenty?"

"Close. One-eighteen."

Hand on the small of my back. I was wearing a loose crop top, low-rise shorts. His fingers swept high, scoping out my shoulder blades. I can get away without a bra, and when he discovered my back was bare, he hesitated. Then he curved his fingertips gently and stroked me in a blatant caress. His nails scattered sparks over my skin, sent shivers pulsing up my spine and across my scalp. My nipples stuck out hard, right in his face. I wanted to push my breast into his mouth. He smiled and tucked a folded bill into my waistband.

"The round's on me. Keep the change, darling. Come down to practice tomorrow. I want to see you work."

Six-thirty sharp. Pink-misted sky, lake a shimmer of pewter, air thick with the late summer smell of damp leaves. A morning for shorts and ballcaps. I caught up to Jack and Don on the boardwalk to the dock, where the young rowers were already waiting. Don went ahead to give practice instructions. Jack turned to me, smiled slowly and said, "Morning, darling." With easy familiarity, he lay an arm across my shoulders, his touch light but electric.

My face was mirrored in his sunglasses so I couldn't read his eyes, but I was ready for him. With a saucy grin, I put my hand on his back waistband, then pushed my fingers down inside his shorts, just to the outward swell of his ass muscles. I raked his flesh, then gave a little pinch. I said, "So what are you, Jack? Six one? Thirty-nine?"

He chuckled. "Close. I'm forty-two. Now get your hand out of there before I make an example of you in front of all these innocent young rowers."

"You wish," I said.

He grinned and shook his head. "Touché, darling."

My senior men's eights folded long limbs into the shell and I stepped into the stern, picked up the rudder lines. We rocked away from the dock.

Don said, "Clare, take them up to Number One and back in ten."

I knew Jack's eyes would be glued on me. I had them around the buoy and back in ten minutes flat.

Don said, "Let's have a longer run now. Easy. Let's say, Number Three, thirtyfour thirty or so."

We sidled back in to the dock spot on time, rocking, shipping their blades neatly.

Don said, "I told you, Jack. Perfect timing."

The junior ladies' eights had gathered on the grass in their pink Speedos, giggling. Jack turned to them and clapped twice, instantly had their rapt attention. We timed them up and back the lake, three heads nodding to our watches at each buoy. I turned to Jack.

"They're good," I said. "They're so disciplined. They've got great rhythm."

A little smile at the corner of his mouth. He said, "You're good, too. Have lunch with me."

Don grinned and said, "Don't get carried away, you two."

At the club cafeteria, he told me he was taking leave from his law practice to coach. He said he liked my work, and that he and Don had agreed I should think about going to Vancouver to cox for the national team. I explained that after I finished my master's degree in naval history, I planned to write a book about ladies' rowing in Canada. I didn't want to interrupt my academic career.

"It would only be for two years," he said.

I said, "I don't know, Jack. I would have to make so many changes. It would take a lot to convince me." He had been looking out over the lake, but suddenly his eyes fixed on me, and his lip curved in a way that made my blood run hot.

He said, "Let me take you for a row."

He handed me into one of the dinghies the club keeps at the far end of the boardwalk for recreational rows. It was a clunky but comfortable craft, perfect for a lazy summer scull. I sat in the stern and closed my eyes, enjoying the lift and lap of the oars in the water, the pleasant surge and dip of the boat under his powerful stroking. I thought of his fingers on my back. I thought of the bulge of his ass. Him, naked. Me naked, with him. I slit my eyes. Imagined straddling him on that seat and pressing myself open right over him. His cock, engorging, would rise straight up into me.

He said, "Do you realize you're moving back and forth with me?"

"Force of habit," I said. Laughing, blushing. "Stroke. Stroke. Now, faster."

Next morning, we were having coffee on the deck after practice.

He reached out and took my hand, fingered my fingers. He said, "No ring, darling? Any boyfriends?"

I said, "Not at the moment. What difference would that make to you anyway?"

"I wouldn't want to displace anyone in your heart."

I laughed. "Bullshit, Jack. I just wonder if you come on to every woman you meet the way you're coming on to me."

His lip curved and I realized my pulse was pounding. "Only the ones with beautiful backs," he said quietly. "Correction: the smart ones with beautiful backs."

He asked me to dinner and I wanted to wear something to knock his damn eyes out. I chose a tight mini-dress in summer white, backless. When we met in the parking lot at the Crow's Nest, he took my hand, made me spin around, couldn't resist stroking my back. He said, "Darling, you clearly want to drive me mad. Excuse my crudity, but you look fucking gorgeous."

Goosebumps rose on my arms. I said, "Sometimes crudity is more than welcome."

He tutted. "She's not only beautiful but bad. A better combination than I ever hoped for."

I laughed. "In your dreams, Jack."

The restaurant was nautical, all polished hardwood railings, illuminated oil portraits of the great ships of history, a big brass bell. A perfect ambience for talking rowing. Over liqueurs I said, "You must have a coaching secret."

He said, "No secret, darling. Common sense. I tell my rowers, all you have to do is give me everything." He put down his glass. "It's all I ever ask of anyone."

I said, "Everything is a lot to ask anyone for."

He said, "Would you ever ask anyone for everything?"

"I don't know. I don't know if I could presume that much. Maybe I would expect them to give it to me anyway."

In the parking lot, while heat lightning flickered in the summer dark, he kissed me gently and said, "Every man in the place wanted to peel this off you."

I asked, "Do you?"

He said, "Slowly. With my teeth."

I swallowed, laughed nervously. "With your teeth. Sounds a little ferocious."

He said softly. "A little ferocity is always fun, darling."

His eyes glittered dangerously. At that moment, I knew it was inevitable. We were going to fuck. And soon.

That night I dreamed he bit into my flesh at my shoulder, tore the skin slowly off my back in long burning strakes, with a sound like fabric ripping to shreds, while I ached for his cock, crying, "I want everything, Jack. Give me everything."

The racing schedule got so busy that I didn't see him again until the team bash on Saturday night. The revelers congregated inside while a thunderstorm raged and the bar lights flickered. Jack sat with Don and the guys, and I found myself sweating under his gaze. In the low light his eyes looked predatory, almost menacing.

Ferocious. I had to force myself to keep the orders straight. I knew exactly what he was thinking about. I hardly dared to think about it, but I couldn't think about anything else.

I was leaning into the bar with a tray of empties when a brilliant flash momentarily threw the power out. Sudden darkness, ear-splitting crack of thunder. I felt his hand on the back of my thigh, creeping up under the leg of my shorts. He squeezed my cheek languidly. Prickles of anticipatory heat bloomed upwards over my ass and between my legs. His lips were on my ear, his jaw bristling against my skin.

"Darling, I am going to fuck you senseless tonight."

Not, *I would like to*. Not, *I want to. Now, do you want me to?* But, *I am going to. Fuck. You. Senseless.* What with the heat, his eyes, his fingers, and his incendiary words, I was throbbing so hard with apprehension and arousal, I thought my heart might burst.

***

Eventually, the crowd thinned. The clouds, still flashing pink, tore and tumbled across a full moon. The storm was clearing. "Come for a row," he said, taking my wrist. There was no getting away. The summer night was steaming with jungle smells.

He pushed off, angled the oars, leaned into his stroke. Relaxed, no rush. He didn't take his eyes off me, that maddening curve in his lip. Even though I was streaming with sweat, my tongue stuck to the roof of my mouth, dust-dry.

In contrast, my pussy was slick and moving. It felt like an animal apart from me, something with its own pulse, life, and destiny. His prey.

He said, "Where can we go that's private?"

I said, "You mean outdoors?"

"Of course, darling," he said quietly. "Ferocity needs a wild setting."

I swallowed and said, "There's a little cove, just around the point over there. Lots of woods."

We beached the punt in bright moonlight. He led me into the dripping shadows under the trees and pressed me back against a trunk with a grinding kiss that left my mouth hanging open, wet.

He slipped off his T-shirt. I watched him stretch it out between his hands, then rotate his wrists to spin it into a long, narrow twist of black cloth. He held it up to me, smiling. "A blindfold," he said. "Are you afraid of it?"

"No," I lied. I was terrified. But I wanted it. Ferocity. I wanted everything he was going to give me.

He tied it tight. Total blackness. For a moment, I almost panicked, my fingers rigid, drawing air, reaching for him. Sensations became isolated, telegraphic. I had to work to string them together and extract meaning.

Hands captured mine. He whispered, "Now, my gorgeous darling. Relax. All you have to do is give me everything."

What happened next was all so tender and deliberate, it was like a dance, a ritual.

He raised my arms gently. He said, "I love this top on you." He slipped it off over my head, eased my arms down. "There. Even better off you."

He drew down my shorts. More slowly, he eased down my thong. Soaked. When it peeled away from my flesh, I felt fiery and overripe, painfully ready to burst. His breath hissed between his teeth. "Darling."

In utter darkness, I felt his eyes all over me, his breathing deafening in the silence. I was skinned alive, my inner flesh fully exposed, gelatinous and trembling, throbbing all over. Bare feet, cold in the damp leaf litter. The invisible pressure of his gaze was agony.

"Jack. Do something. Touch me."

Clink of belt buckle. Zipper. Rustle of clothing, dropping. Naked now.

He said, "Turn around."

I longed to see him, leaf-dappled in moonlight. He approached behind. His cock brushed my hip, silky. Upright and rock-hard. Mouth on my shoulder. Trail of kisses to my ass, lingering.

He whispered, "Around. Again."

He was kneeling. He lifted my thigh to his shoulder. Mouth on me.

"Open wide, darling. Wider." I tipped, caught myself against a tree.

Fingers drawing my folds apart. Lips, tongue, open mouth pressed gently, then harder, sucking my flesh slowly to a pulp, into streams running down over his chin. "Oh Jack." I came with my fingers clenched in his hair.

He made me lie face-down, full-length in wet fleshy leaves,

spongy moss and leaf-mould, slime of squashed mushrooms on my cheek. He stretched my arms out overhead and tied me to a tree with his belt. Taking his time.

"So you can brace yourself," he said. I noticed an edge of excitement in his voice. "So you can't get away from me. Now pull up your knees. Stick your ass in the air."

I hesitated.

He said, "Stick your fucking ass up. Right now."

His urgency alarmed me. I complied. Upended, exposed, quaking with desire and dread.

Touch. One hand sliding in from the front, thumb seeking my clit, fingers moving deep inside. One hand kneading my ass, spreading my cheeks with finger and thumb. Cold air into me. Stubble, scraping. His mouth, sliding. One wildly pulsating spot. I gasped. His mouth was right there. A kiss, lips, opening. "Jesus. Jack. No."

Tongue. Circle and probe. "No, no."

"Yes," he said.

Fingertip. Touch. Press. Harder. There was pleasure winding to the breaking point, now unfurling, uncoiling towards me like a mountainous wave. "Oh, Jack, don't."

I tried to crawl away, struggled against my bonds.

He pulled me backwards, hard.

A shockwave of fire burst from his finger and radiated outwards along all my nerves, electrifying me, exploding from my anus to the roots of my hair and out to the tips of my fingers and toes. Sweat must have sprayed out of me like mist. My thigh muscles liquefied and my clit felt like a huge, pulsing marble under his thumb. My nipples throbbed, hard as bullets. Maybe I screamed. It occurred to me that I was dying. His relentless hands were shaping me into a river of molten flesh and I was flowing ecstatically into oblivion.

I sagged away, and he moved in close behind, kneed my legs open, nudged. Fumbled.

"Lift up," he growled. "Open the fuck up."

In a daze, I arched my spine until it cramped, offered myself to him, thighs trembling. He fingered me open, then sank deep, hard. Ferocious. Animal. I thought of the savage mating of tigers, how the male bites and restrains the female with his claws flexed into her sides, how she snarls and pushes back, vicious in her heat. I grasped the tree and shoved my hips back to meet him, impaling myself as he slammed into me.

Stroke. Stroke. Stroke, faster. Harder. I was no match for his strength. My arms buckled. My mouth ploughed open into spongy ground. He pounded me until he collapsed and I went limp in a hail of stars.

As if from above, floating, I saw our limbs, sprawled and spent, torsos faintly glowing in the moonlight, slick with sweat, dirtied with litter of the forest floor. As if we had just erupted from the soil, blossomed overnight like some strange and radiant fungoid, the pallid flower of a furious and subterranean coupling.

My chin, elbows, nipples, knees, were rubbed raw. My mouth was full of the taste of earth. The residue of our ferocity.

We dipped in the dark shimmering lake, dried off in the dinghy. He pulled my head onto his thigh, water lipping my heel cast lazily over the side. I fingered his cock, clammy, soft and so sweetly innocuous my mouth watered for it.

He said, "I want you in Vancouver."

He pulled me up for a kiss. I knelt on the seat and straddled him. I felt his bulk, soft, then stirring. He smiled, pressed his hands into my back. "What do I have to do to convince you?"

"I don't know, Jack. I don't know."

THE STORY HER BODY TOLD
by August MacGregor

No one answered Jason's knock. The door was unlocked, so he let himself in and called out: "Hello?" No answer. Strange. Out here on a posh estate in beautiful Virginia horse country, you'd think that someone would be watching the house.

Usually, Isabel answered the door. Jason thought a butler dressed in coat and tails and speaking with an English accent would be nice. That would match Mr. Needlesham and his English airs, even though Jason was suspicious that they were fake.

But neither the maid nor the master of the house were in sight today. So long as the mistress was here, that's all that really counted.

Jason called out again, decided what the hell, and entered the house. It was an odd feeling, of being an intruder, amid the quiet and stillness of the antique furniture. Mr. Needlesham—in the painting of him and his wife above the fireplace —stared down at Jason with menacing eyes.

He made his way to the kitchen, yelling "hello" several times, but still receiving no answer. After coming here for many months, he was familiar with the house. He had been very impressed his first time at the place. Once he'd pulled off the road and passed through the break in the rock wall, the estate opened up before him, with its plush green lawn, small pond, white wooden fences, and woods that stretched to the mountains. The large front doors were each carved with the Skyward crest: a shield containing a hawk with folded wings, a banner swirling and curling on both sides.

Mr. Needlesham, a tall man with a thick gray moustache, had met Jason at the door that time and shook his hand with a firm grip. On the house tour, Jason was introduced to the finery: Oriental rugs, paintings of the countryside and hunting dogs, antiques of dark wood with beautiful patina (he could not resist touching the smooth satin finish), and wall colors of burgundy, forest green, buttery yellow.

Throughout the tour, Mr. Needlesham had carried himself with the air of one who was used to getting what he wanted. A breezy confidence. He spoke with no English accent, but he sprinkled his speech with tidbits like "brilliant" and "chap." He explained that he was a semi-retired lawyer who still had cases back at the firm in Georgetown.

Their conversation in the den was memorable, surrounded by bookcases full of old volumes and a huge world map hanging on one wall. Jason pictured Mr. Needlesham easing into one of the dark brown leather chairs, teeth clenching a pipe, and dreaming of global domination.

"There was," Mr. Needlesham had said, "a woman here before. But Amy thought her too ... soft. So it is time to try a masseur. By your handshake, I can tell you have strong hands." Under the man's gaze, Jason felt as if he were being sized up, judged like a potential juror to see if he would be beneficial to the case. "Treat her with care. She tells me that massages release her tensions and toxins in her muscles. She treats her body like a temple."

Then Amy had entered the den. Immediately, Jason wanted to touch the denim of her jeans, the wool of her sweater, the silk of her long red hair. Then peel away her clothes to brush against the soft underwear (small floral print, he guessed) and peel that away until there was only skin, beautiful and supple skin.

The refrigerator's loud hum brought him back to the present. In the kitchen, Jason wished for Amy's presence and fun personality to break this quiet. He checked his watch at the back door and took a moment to enjoy the view from the windows: trees meeting mountains, one lined after another and fading from green to blue-gray.

Being alone in the house got to him. He figured he would wait a few minutes outside then leave. He retraced his steps to his car, reached through the driver's window and honked the horn a couple times.

Then he heard the dogs barking somewhere in the woods. Two golden retrievers appeared from the trees and bounded over the lawn toward him. Upon reaching him, they wagged their tails and sniffed his legs.

Scratching the back of their necks, Jason called them by name—Ivan and Heidi—and heard a horse trotting toward them.

A voice yelled: "Jason!"

Not the master of the house, but the mistress. Jason had never seen her on horseback before. She acted as if it was second nature, moving with the animal's muscular strides.

"Jason," she said. "I'm so sorry. I lost track of time."

Closer now, he could see that she was wearing a white shirt and blue jeans— not exactly the traditional riding outfit that most in the area wore. Her glossy black boots made his blood run faster. Mud flecked her boots and jeans. Sweat beaded her forehead. Auburn hair was tied in a ponytail.

"No problem," he said, still enchanted, even after the many massages he had given her. "No need to apologize. Is Mr. Needlesham out riding too?"

"He's away on business for a few days. And I gave Isabel and Ben a couple of days off. It's so quiet, but it's wonderfully quiet. Nice to have a break by myself. Go ahead and set up your things. I'll be ready in a few minutes."

She turned and rode off for the stables, the dogs in hot pursuit.

So they were alone. Gone were the husband, maid, and cook. Jason was reminded of some Agatha Christie book involving a murder deep in the English countryside. He laughed, but gave himself a serious warning: *Watch your step, buddy. Don't try anything that you'll regret. When are you going to massage a woman like this again? Plus, this client pays way too well to lose.*

He took a few moments to let that thought really sink in and enjoy the sight of Amy riding away, then lugged the massage table and backpack to the second floor of the house. Their usual place was a sort of dressing room, just off the stair landing, with one entrance from the hall and another to the walk-in closet and, beyond that, the master bathroom. He unfolded the table and unpacked his CD player and oils.

While hearing the shower through the second door, he wondered what she would do if he joined her. He could give her a shower rub-down, concentrating the soap suds on her breasts and pussy, then she would reach for his hard cock... but he had to stop the fantasy. Over the past several months, he had lusted for her—and massages twice a week made it worse. But he was afraid of losing her as a client. Any unwanted advances, and she might kick him out for good. Then his hands and eyes would miss this beautiful creature.

The inner door opened, and she entered in a white terrycloth robe. Hair still dripped, smile lit up his day as it always did.

"Don't rush," he said. "There's no need. Remember, this is all about you relaxing."

She said, "It's just that I hate being late. You probably have a schedule, and I don't want to mess that up. Have I made you late for your next appointment?"

"Not at all," he lied and mentally noted to call the next

client, the middle-aged Mrs. Miller, and tell her that, so sorry, he had a flat tire. "We have all the time you need. Please." He gestured with both hands to the table.

She began untying the robe's sash and he turned to look out the window.

She chided him: "You always do that. And you always see me naked on the table anyway. Why is that?"

"It's the act of undressing. It's too...what's the word I want? 'Intimate.'"

During their first massage, Jason had covered her breasts and groin with towels—his way of respecting a client's privacy. On the second time, she had wanted to remove the towels, saying they got in the way and she preferred the all-body massage. Seeing her ripe breasts, he wasn't about to complain and was glad her eyes were closed so she wouldn't catch him staring. When his hands got to the mounds, he forced restraint and professional behavior upon his fingers. Ever since, he had kept close watch on his hands should they attempt a mutiny. Same with his erection. With closed eyes, she never saw him pitching a tent, and he was careful not to rub his groin against her.

Touching her felt like he was creeping to the edge of an affair with a gorgeous woman he could never have. To him, not only was she on a different stratum, like cheerleaders in high school, but married to boot. Still, he wanted to ravage her.

He busied himself by hitting 'play' on his CD player, starting soft music of Japanese flute and wind chimes, and selecting two oils: ylang-ylang and sandalwood. He dripped them on his palms, rubbed the palms together, and thought, *What the hell is ylang-ylang anyway?* The combination smelled rich and musky.

"I'm ready," she said. "You can turn around now." She was on the table, settling into a comfortable position on her back. "One of these days, you'll have to be naked, too. It's only fair."

He was caught off guard—was she teasing him? His brain quickly collected scattered words, and his mouth stumbled over them: "If you, uh, wish...that could be arranged."

"What of my other wishes?" Her eyes were shut, but there was a ghost of a smile.

Gaining composure, he said, "My lady, you are my gracious employer. I am here to do your bidding." He thought, *Carefully play the game, but watch it, pal.*

The ghost materialized into a real smile. "Good to know. Right now, I want to be relaxed. Do your handiwork."

He started kneading her shoulders, smiling at the freckles on them. Then he reached underneath her neck to the middle of her spine and, pressing his fingers up against her muscles, dragged them back toward him. Her body eased and she sighed, ready for the journey.

And so it began. He slowed his breathing to follow hers and pushed while exhaling. His palms and fingers worked, reading the story her body told. Her buttery smooth skin with its characters of muscles (the basement of the house held gym equipment, which she must have used regularly), freckles, a birthmark, two tattoos, and a couple of small scars were all familiar to him.

The birthmark was on the back of her right thigh. Mostly it reminded Jason of a cloud, but sometimes of a fox.

The small tattoo on her left ankle was a small heart, the ink faded and worn. Perhaps she had gotten it years ago in the midst of drunken spring break revelry. The other, fresher and brighter, was the Skyward crest on her lower back. It surprised him when he first saw it, and made him wonder if it was meant as a brand on one of Mr. Needlesham's possessions or a sign of her dedication to him or something else entirely.

There were only two scars—one on her right foot and one on her right knee. Jason guessed they were from riding accidents, similar to the time she bruised her left knee. The massages had continued, and Amy had asked him to come more frequently while she recuperated, believing that his work helped the knee to heal.

The story, as always, had a lusty side. Hovering over her breasts slick with oil, his hands desired to squeeze, not rub. But his palms relinquished, instead moving in figure 8's around her breasts, then flat on top of them, rubbing in circular motions. His tongue wanted to trace the bumps of her areola, and his cock ached to slide between them. Another destination also beckoned. If only his fingers could dive into her pubic hair then slip down and caress the folds of her pussy: his tongue could travel around and play with her clitoris, his nose could sniff her sweet smell mixing with the musk and ylang-ylang—all before the finale of his cock parting the folds and being engulfed by her warm flesh.

Again he envied Mr. Needlesham. But had to hand it to the old guy—he had good taste. Estate in the country, beautiful wife—shame the old rich guys get women of this quality. And with Viagra, the old man could give and give all night long. Still, Jason wondered if Amy was satisfied. She was, after all, half Mr. Needlesham's age. Maybe less. And here was Jason, on the unwrinkled side of 50.

But Mr. Needlesham struck an imposing presence, even an imaginary one. Jason pictured him in a blacksmith's shop, angry flames behind him, soot smeared across bare chest, black leather apron to his ankles. He was beating a piece of metal on the anvil, then picked it up, showed Jason the pike with red-hot point, and said in a Sean Connery voice, "Try something, old chap, and you'll get this up yer arse."

Jason could not find any obvious cameras recording his every move, although he didn't put it past the old man. And the eyes in the painting didn't move. It was of Amy sitting on the beach, hair and sundress caught in the ocean breeze, and a lighthouse in the background. It was much better than the one above the fireplace, of Mr. Needlesham looking stern in a gray suit and Amy looking serious in a black dress, but with a touch of humor as if gently laughing at the painter with spinach on a tooth.

He went back to focusing on his technique. Eventually, his hands slowed to deeper rubs and gradually eased to a stop. Unfortunately, the hour was up—even though he could touch her all day and night.

With closed eyes and steady breathing, she seemed completely relaxed. Often she looked as if asleep—hypnotized and soothed by the massage.

He tiptoed out of the room, closing the door softly behind him. He would wait five minutes in the hallway to give her time to transition and leave through the inner door. Then he would pack his stuff and run to the next appointment.

The house was quieter than usual. One of the golden retrievers—Ivan—drowsily shuffled in, sniffed Jason, accepted a few scratches, then left to return to the living room's sunspot for more slumber.

Usually, Isabel showed up as she heard the door open and close, then would come and make small talk. But her real purpose was probably to keep tabs on him and make sure he didn't pocket any valuables. Not this time, though. After Ivan left, his only companion was the grandfather clock, and it was telling no stories. Just letting him know when five minutes were up.

He opened the door and was shocked.

There Amy stood, completely naked, skin glistening with massage oil. Hair loose on her shoulders. Riding crop in hand. Eyes playful.

Mouth agape, he must have looked like a silly cartoon.

"Now, about those wishes," she said.

His heart leapt into a higher gear, blood hurtling toward his dick.

"First, the clothes," she commanded.

Practically stumbled out his clothes. Standing naked with pounding chest, he reminded himself of a starved animal in sight of meat. *Not a romantic image,* he thought, *but then again, neither is that riding crop.*

She tossed it across the room. Reflexes enabled him to catch it, his brain too busy with savagery to send impulses to merely catch something. The black leather handle felt nicely balanced with the long slick stem and flat head.

For a moment she looked him over, slightly smiling at his quizzical look. Then she descended to the white robe splayed out on the floor and moved to all fours so she faced away from him.

Still deep in disbelief, he simply stared at her sweet ass.

She turned to look at him, flashing her fiery eyes, and asked, "Going to stand there all day?"

Logical thoughts actually made their way through the fog: *Screw losing a client. Screw Mr. Needlesham—well, not literally. Time to screw this girl. Gotta make the customer happy.* Heart racing, he walked to her and gently swatted her ass with the riding crop.

"That won't do," she said. "Oh, wait—you don't ride horses. Jason, dear, you'll have to go a shade harder."

He tried, with a little more force.

"Better," she said.

Then again, and the flat leather head slapped her ass cheek louder. Waited, feeling like an eager school boy.

"Even better. Now, keep it up."

He followed, and was surprised about how much it was turning him on. An old girlfriend, in a bubbly and tipsy mood, had suggested that he spank her. A few gentle blows had satisfied her, for she flipped to her back and pulled his cock to her.

That was play; this felt much different. Yet a touch more strength, the slap louder. "Mmmmm," Amy said.

He alternated cheeks, hitting with the same force and trying not to swing too hard. She lowered to rest on her forearms, her right hand masturbating herself.

Several more hits and he couldn't resist any longer. He knelt behind her and as he entered her, she immediately pushed against him, sliding his cock deep into her. He realized he was panting, so he commanded his lungs to breathe slower; over-excitement might lead to an early finish. His hips slowly rocked, pulling his shaft out of her, then pushing all of himself back inside her hot wetness. She began to moan, softly at first, then increasing as he spanked her with his hand.

The scene below amazed him. Was this really happening? The body that he had touched so many times before, now it moved against him, in rhythm with his cock sliding in her pussy. Over and over he thought, *Oh my God, I'm actually fucking her.* The Skyward crest tattoo on her lower back, once a familiar curiosity, was now strangely erotic as he wanted to brand his own crest on her ass with his hot come. The pinkness of her cheeks fascinated him. He almost requested a mirror to place in front of her so he could see her face. But that would mean stopping. And pulling out.

Their bodies swayed, both lost in the movement and feeling. His hips were a steady piston; her fingers rubbed circles on her clitoris. Her moans were louder now, her thighs more energetic in pushing against him, her fingers faster, moans building up and up to skyward.... Until she reached the clouds and climaxed.

Her left arm slid to the side so that her face rested on the robe, her ass now arched higher, her body trembled, her moans shifted into heavy pants. He bent forward, hands gliding under her stomach, lifted her slightly and, finding her breasts, finally (after all these months!) squeezed the ripe globes. His fingers practically broke out in song. His breath and hips moved faster, as he imagined his cock a hard leather riding crop, lust pulsed through his veins, any sense of time thrown out of the window, the world now condensed down to his cock in her pussy, her tits filling his strong hands, and moans, him wanting more and more to never stop.

But he did.

Ejaculated in hard surges, releasing months of pent-up craving.

Afterward, he was surprised by how tightly he was holding her breasts, so he relaxed his grip. His hands would not let go, not just yet, not after waiting so long.

Their chests heaving, their bodies slowed their sex rhythm.

Again, he gazed down in wonder and when she turned to meet his eyes, giving him a pleased and contented look, the longing returned for the next time he could touch her.

NUDE DREAMS OR NAKED REALITY?
by Steven Fire

Leering eyes danced over Jenna's skin. She covered her breasts with one arm and her groin with the other. Frantic, she tried to think of a rational reason as to why she sat naked in the lecture hall. Jenna forced a smile for one guy, but still felt the need to cover.

"Can I borrow your coat?" she asked the girl next to her.

"It's your own fault for coming to class naked like that," retorted the girl.

The professor stared at her. "Thank you for the thrill, young lady. But this isn't California."

Jenna feigned a laugh with the crowd. Still unsure of how she'd ended up this way, and unable to tell what lecture hall she sat in, Jenna decided to leave. When she stood, cat-calls whistled from the guys. Her cold, embarrassed skin shrank from prying eyes. Nipples hardened as an indescribable electric rush cascaded through her body. Jenna wished she had not chosen to sit in front of the class. Both embarrassed and turned on, Jenna did not know how to react. Just get out. Someone slapped her ass. Trying to laugh, Jenna continued climbing the cold stairs. They took forever. Just how big *was* the classroom?

Breaking into a run, Jenna wished she had a third hand to cover her butt. Excited, scared, intense, Jenna climbed faster. Confused, Jenna now stood on the grassy lawn in front of dorms.

How the fuck did I get here?

Light interplayed with shade too fast and quick. The people moved in strange fashion—almost like stop-motion photography.

People stared. Jenna covered herself again. The dorms all looked alike. Which one was hers? Turning south, she ran again, still hearing the cat-calls. A camera flashed. "This one's for the promotional calendar!"

Jenna screamed.

Another bulb flashed. "For my closet wall."

Jenna needed to get away. Finally arriving inside the dorm, she made her way toward the elevator. Another camera caught her nudity.

"This one's for the Internet."

Jenna stepped onto the elevator with six or seven other students. Stupefied, they scanned every inch of her nudity. Closing her eyes, she wished them away. *What is taking this elevator so long? Don't panic*, she told herself, *you just gotta get to the fifth floor.* The fourth bell rang. The elevator, which now seemed larger with more people, stopped. The motor stopped running. Stuck, she desperately punched the buttons. "No! Not now." Jenna shrank into a corner, feeling the eyes of everyone stare at her. Again, liking and hating the attention, Jenna savored the combination of humiliation and horniness. *This is not happening*, she told herself over and over.

Jenna's eyes bolted open. Shaking, breathing heavy, she hugged herself. Feeling her sweat-soaked night-clothes underneath the covers calmed Jenna's nerves. Still, her skin tingled. Excited, definitely aroused, she wondered how an embarrassing nightmare could ignite her sexual appetite.

A boring, monotonous voice lulled Jenna to sleep. Fighting the heavy eyelids, she yawned and shook her head. *How am I going to do at swim practice if I can't stay awake?* Losing her train of thought, she glanced at someone else's notes. Recalling the last main point, Jenna scribbled more notes. A blurry haze outlined the periphery. Resting her chin in one hand, Jenna felt her eyes close.

Gunshot!

Jenna jumped into the pool. The cold, heavy water seemed thicker today. Jenna worked harder to propel her body. Arms hit the soupy water hard as her feet kicked faster. Nearing the end, she flipped and hit the wall, the push-off into stroking worked perfectly. Only reacting, Jenna breathed every six strokes like clockwork. Every gasp provided extra strength to fight the long Olympic-sized pool.

Anticipating the end of the race, Jenna's arms moved faster, slicing the water and propelling her through. Not knowing the place of her competitors, Jenna concentrated on finishing the race. Hitting the wall, she lifted her head and took in a full breath. A hand reached down and Jenna took hold. Eased out of the pool, and realizing her victory, Jenna lifted her arms as the crowed cheered. Quickly, she covered her naked breasts and hunched over. Her skin, cold and wet, felt unworthy of attention. Blushing, anxiety swelled in her chest.

I could have sworn I had on my swimsuit when I started!

Competitors screamed at her. "It's not fair!" They yelled repeatedly "She has to wear a swimsuit. She distracted us!"

Although her teammates surrounded her for congratulations, Jenna felt the need to hide. Moving through them, she tried to find a door—*any* door to seek refuge. None existed. The judges surrounded her, forcing her to the platform. All she wanted was to run and cover herself. Finally, stepping on the top platform, the chief judge placed a gold medal over her head and around her neck. Nipples hardened instantly. Skin warmed and softened. Jenna shook as the old man stared luridly at her flesh. Cameras flashing, she smiled as her teeth chattered.

Holy Shit, she thought. *I finally win the gold and I'm naked.*

Jenna forced her eyelids open. Clutching her chest, she huffed heavily. Quickly, she checked to make sure she wore clothes. Although relieved, Jenna smiled, liking the idea of being the only one naked at a swim meet.

Taking her head off her hand, Jenna flinched—seeing she was the only one left in class. She quickly left.

Jenna worked hard at her aerobics. Although huge drops of sweat seeped through her pours, Jenna felt invigorated. Shoulders, arms, legs—even her ass muscles burned. Feeling confident, powerful, and sexy, Jenna kept pace. The dance instructor accelerated the moves. Jenna pushed aside the weariness, fighting the urge to stop or slow down. Pushing herself, she had to finish with the rest of the aerobics class.

Up the step, down the step. Step to the side, march it out. Step to the other side, march it out. Up the step, down the step. Focusing on the movements and timing, Jenna forgot the aches and pains.

"Okay!" yelled the instructor. "That's it! Give yourselves a hand."

Jenna wiped some sweat off her forehead and clapped. A young man passed behind Jenna. "Thanks for the motivation," he said while slapping her on the bare ass.

Oh no. Not again. Jenna cringed as most of the women rolled their eyes at her.

"Forget something, honey?" asked one girl.

"I hate girls like you," bitched an out-of-shape student.

A few guys gathered close, complimenting Jenna on her body. Deep inside, she enjoyed the attention. A tickling force rushed through her groin. Breathing heavy, Jenna noticed the power of every sensation. At the same time, she desired to stop the prying eyes.

Jenna covered her breasts and crotch, widening her eyes and trying to smile. How do I keep getting into this mess? Bolting out of the aerobics class, she rushed towards the women's locker room. Strangely, the free weights gym blocked her way. It wasn't there before! The locker rooms rested on the other side. She could see them through the glass doors.

Frantic, frenzied, she rushed through the weight room. The rewarding freedom fired Jenna's wild heart—and poisoned her nerves. Unable to tell where the exciting tickling ended and the anxious knots began, Jenna quickened her pace. Men dropped their weights, staring at her bare flesh. A few of them let out whistles, while others threw their comments.

"Hey, want to work me out?"

"You're the reason I went through puberty."

"Just stay and work out, babe."

Jenna tried to smile, and even said "hi" to a few people. Desperate to cover herself, she ran faster. Reaching the other side, Jenna rushed through a locker room door, then cowered next to a locker. Two figures passed by. Jenna felt them gawking at her. Covering herself, she screamed as the two men leered. She was in the guys' locker room!

Jenna awakened in her dorm room. A gentle tingle subtly resonated through her. Jenna caressed her breasts slowly. Soon, her breath shortened as her skin felt the cool sheets and the soft pillows. Sounds of the ticking clock mixed with her heartbeat, rendering a hypnotic affect.

Unable to take it any longer, Jenna reached between her thighs. Stroking her clit forced her eyes shut. Fire swelled, spreading with every stroke. Hands explored her soft, silken stomach, then moved to her breasts. Carefully, she twisted her nipples between her fingers—then used her fingernails to rake them.

Jenna looked inside, trying to find the mixed, euphoric feelings of her dreams. They peaked her sensuality, drawing her closer to orgasm. Not imagining any particular man, she centered on the humiliation. Losing thought, Jenna's hand moved instinctively. Fingers meticulously touched every inch of bare skin and kneaded breasts. One fingernail traced her sternum down her stomach and to her pussy. Reaching inside, Jenna pushed the fingers in and out, up and down, and side to side. Tickling herself, Jenna felt the sexual energy build. It spread out evenly from her crotch, to her stomach, and hips.

Dizziness set in as Jenna worked faster. Gyrating hips combined with searching hands, absorbed and locked in self passion. Moaning, Jenna arched her back, trying to build the energy to its needed level. The sexual vibe reached a plateau, neither finding growth—nor release. Jenna bit her lip, trying to control her symphony of sensual euphoria.

The passion exploded, passing energy into every organ, every limb, and every muscle. At first, everything contracted. Almost instantly, the sexual energy acted like a sedative, taking away every tense knot. Panting, Jenna had to catch her breath.

I gotta do something about these dreams.

Jenna stepped into the bathroom. Putting the backpack on the floor, Jenna removed her top. Breasts dangled freely, savoring the cool ventilation. She took off her shorts and thong, and her bare skin shivered excitedly.

"Jenna?" said Monica. "What are you doing?"

"I've been having these dreams lately," Jenna said while rolling her clothes in her backpack, "...I always end up naked everywhere. The gym, class, swimming. Afterwards, I wake-up turned on, so I'm trying the real thing—and going into the cafeteria like this." Nervous, worried, scared, her breath shortened.

"But you're naked!"

Hiding the fear, Jenna tried to be cavalier while hoisting the backpack over a shoulder. "No I'm not. I'm wearing sandals."

Jenna pinched herself. *Not* dreaming. Putting one hand on the door, she took a deep breath. Here goes nothing...literally....

STRIPPED DOWN
by Jesse Nelson

I stared at myself in the dressing room mirror, listening to the clucks of approval from the obsequious clerk standing behind me. In a haughty tone, he claimed the suit fit me "to perfection," but when I looked, all I saw was a pinstriped gray wool automaton. Didn't seem right to me, even though the outfit was as expensive as all hell. Money can't buy style. I learned that early on. Most people haven't got a handle on that one yet.

"You don't like the cut, Sir?" the clerk asked, concern furrowing his handsome brow. He was obviously envisioning his swiftly vanishing commission.

I shook my head. I couldn't easily explain what was wrong. Yet I knew that the outfit was not in the least bit festive. Not at all unique. But what did I expect, after all? I'd come to a place where people paid to look like everyone else. The uniform was chic enough; that didn't make a difference in this case. I stripped down and put my own clothes back on— Levis, T-shirt, and sweater. Now, I looked like me again, but this wasn't the right attire, either. Finally, I decided I'd have to bring Glenda into the deliberations. My girlfriend has an uncanny style sense, and this was *her* friend's party, after all. I'd been trying to prove to myself—and to her—that I had enough know-how to put together an outfit. But I proved wrong.

Glenda was thrilled to be asked. "Don't worry, Tommy," she told me. "I have the perfect place to take you."

I should have been wary. And I should have known exactly where she'd take me. One of her all-time favorite stores, down the street from her apartment on Melrose, an upscale consignment emporium overflowing with finery from days gone by. Or, more honestly, from the 70s. When I saw the wide ties and the polka dotted shirts, the fake fur and the plaid—oh, Jesus, the plaid—I almost turned around. Glenda had a firm grip on me, and she pushed me forward.

"Not my style," I told her.

"You promised to trust me," she responded.

Generally, I'm about suits or Levis. I work as a lawyer in a conservative practice. Can't get away with scuffed shoes at the office, even in California. Glenda's in the movies, a costume designer on the biggest-budget endeavors. She adds class to any scene, adds considerable style points even to me, just by being on my arm. Now I was putting myself in her knowledgeable hands—why did that freak me out?

While I teetered on the verge of losing my cool, Glenda busied herself gathering armloads of clothes. Then, after shooting me an "I'm ready" look, she herded me into the dressing room ahead of her. I hated everything she'd chosen. Wasn't me. Wasn't my scene. But I forced a patient expression onto my face and tried each outfit she presented me with. Couldn't she see how uncomfortable I was in the baggy pants and suspenders? The skinny tie and rock-a-billy shirt? The dyed black denims with stove pipe legs? Didn't she know that my general look is not only one of convenience but one of comfort? I like to blend in. That's precisely what my uniform does for me. Turns me into part of the crowd.

Of course, she understood. That's why she was having so much fun. With her orange and purple numbers, the swirls and patterns, she was in a psychedelic dream come true. "Relax, Tommy," she hissed at me. "You're not having a good time at all, only because you've got that stick up your ass."

"This ass?" I said, posing for her in my BVDs. "That's what you think the trouble is?"

She stifled a laugh. "I know *that's* not the trouble." She took a moment to admire my rear view. "But you have to start letting go a little. This is a costume party, after all. You can't wear a suit and be a lawyer."

"But that's who I am."

"Exactly. The costume part of the party means dressing up as something you're not." She said this with a bit of exasperation, as if she couldn't understand why I wouldn't do things her way. Part of the reason we're such a good couple is that we're so different—but every once in awhile, our headstrong ways meet in the middle and we find we can neither go forward nor back.

Which is when she got the idea. I could see it happening, her eyes widening, her mouth parting. "Why didn't I think of that earlier?" she cooed to herself, pushing the pile of clothing aside.

"What do you mean?"

"Trust me," she said again, leading me from the store and back up the hill to her place. "Just trust me."

In her apartment, she let me watch her dress herself. She was going as Eve, with well-placed fig leaves strategically hiding her most lovely assets. Then she blindfolded me and told me to stand up in front of her. This wasn't the first time we'd played sensory deprivation games, but it was the first time we did so outside of a strictly sexual situation. Maybe that's why I got hard so quickly. I felt slippery garments moving over my body, felt her angling and arranging items to suit her. I wished I could see, but Glenda said no, and when she says no, I listen. That's another reason why we're such a good team. At home, behind closed doors, she's the one in charge. It's always been that way with us, and I revel in giving up my power to her, and all the insane complications that power brings with it.

She took me in her car, still wearing the blindfold, and then drove us in near silence for twenty minutes. The only sounds were the traffic around us and Glenda's occasional murmurings to herself, snippets of song lyrics that she had a habit of singing—out of nowhere—Bono. Dylan. The Stones.

Finally, she parked and ushered me, still blindfolded, into the party. It was at a mansion, way up in the hills. I could tell from the noise level, the mixtures of expensive perfume and scent of alcohol in the air, that the place was crushed with people. I heard them stop when we entered.

There she goes again, I thought. *My Glen, cutting a scene.*

I felt her remove my overcoat, and then I felt her fingers working rapidly. A gust of warm air rushed against me, and I thought I understood.

But no—she wouldn't have done that, would she?

Oohs and ahhs sounded immediately around us, and Glenda took my hand and moved me into midst of the partiers. Again, I thought *that* thought. The unthinkable thought. I could feel fabric. I wasn't naked. Was I?

"So lovely, Glenny," someone cooed to her.

"You've done it again."

"A masterpiece."

I grabbed onto the blindfold, but Glenda hissed at me. "Stop, or I won't reward you. Tonight will be a lonely, pleasureless night if you disobey me." So I allowed her to take me, still blind, through her entire scene, until she felt the location was right. Only then, did she tell me I could remove the scarf. When she did, I found that we were in the master bathroom, in a room of mirrors, wall upon wall of mirrors. And I found that yes, I was naked, and no, I was not. She'd put me in a gauzy layer of entirely sheer fabric. A suit of nothing.

A naked suit.

The story came together in my head suddenly: The Emperor's New Clothes, with each fawning attendee ooohing and ahhing over something that wasn't there at all. And yet in this story, the lack of clothing wasn't a cruel trick, or an evil surprise, but the best gift my girlfriend could ever have given me. Because suddenly the door opened and the partiers hurried in, as many as could fit in the room, and there were hands on me, and mouths on me, open and kissing me, fingers probing, skin on skin.

I felt the rustling rush of a fresh mouth on my cock, and I looked to see Glenda urging a lovely young starlet to drink me down. She was blonde and winsome with a peony-painted mouth that she parted wide in order to grant me access. As I felt the wet heat of her mouth close around my rod, I turned my to see the prettiest brunette begin working her pussy in front of me, hitched up on the marble counter, legs spread, letting me watch as she teased herself on toward a magnificent orgasm. Another couple began to fuck right next to me, their bodies so close, their emotions so raw. I could feel their breaths, sense their shudders and shivers of each forward thrust.

My eyes were in constant motion, trying to drink in every erotic image that whirred around me. The spike-haired boy going down on his girlfriend in the marble shower. The handsome older man instructing a svelte redhead in the interesting uses of the bidet. Glenda suddenly pushed the startled ingenue out of the way, and she took her rightful position on the floor, sucking me hard, all the way down to the root so that her lips pressed against my skin. I liked that her lipstick was smeared, even though I hadn't seen her kissing anyone. I liked that she didn't have a problem swapping spit with the vixen who'd been locked to my cock only moments before.

I liked it all.

She deep-throated me like a pro, and I had to put my hands out for a moment, feeling dizzy with the pleasure, finding it an effort simply to stay standing, to remain in an upright and locked position. Immediately, several partiers came to my aid, moving closer, supporting me with their own bodies, keeping me steady so that I could enjoy every second of Glenda blowing me in front of all those people. All those curious, watching, ravenous people.

And I got. Suddenly, I got it.

Stripped down, and *un*dressed, without the comfort and safety of my standard uniform, I felt more free than I ever have before.

NAKED AMBITION
by Savannah Stephens Smith

I fucked my way to the top.

Not many women admit that these days, if they ever did. But I'm sure, despite changes in how we look at men and women, work and power, that a lot of women—and maybe some men, too—still do it. You grab your chances any way you can, and what's offered up in return is old and compelling. And oh, so hard to resist.

Maybe fewer have to do it these days. Times have changed, even in the business world. Me, I liked to fuck, and I had no commitments at home. I could have. I'm not gorgeous, but I am just fine. But I was also a busy woman with a career that meant a lot to me. My job was my life. I didn't have much patience for nonsense, wasting time in boring bars, being coy with a straw, hunting for Mr. Right. *Mr. Right Now* would do. And my belief was that if a good lay was going to give me pleasure and get me ahead, I'd take that over Joe in the corner any time. If a shortcut's available, there's no point in driving all over the country to get to where you really want to be.

And I wanted to be at the top. Who doesn't?

Fucking. As a strategy, it's as old as time, and it seems as effective now as it was an eon ago when Oga found that putting out for Og got her a warmer spot by the fire and a little extra grilled sabre-tooth, to boot. It's human, as human as we all are, and I won't apologize for it, even now.

Sex is something we all do, all want, except for priests and the hopeless. And we've seen what happens when men's desires are sublimated. They turn dark and twisted. It's not healthy to deny your lusts.

And we all have desires, sometimes buried, sometimes right out in the open. And one of my gifts is for knowing desire, for finding it, no matter how hidden. It's like holding a narrow, forked branch in your hands, taken from the earth. Closing your eyes, and just feeling the song in the ground, and there knowing where the water lies. And gentlemen, some of you run deep. And strange.

So there you have it, what you all suspected is true: I fucked my way to the top.

Of course, some of you know that already. Just like some of you know just how I liked my fun along the way. Some men are so grateful to get a bit, and to get it from a good-looking woman with a few brains in her head, too. For heaven's sake, some of you acted like you'd won the lottery, and all I had to do was indulge in something I wanted to do anyway.

Because some of you know me well. Very well. Don't fidget, Stanley, I enjoyed our mornings together. And I don't blame you for giving me the best assignments. That's what friends do for each other. And I wasn't lying when I told you that you knew how to please me like no other man.

I still remember—especially now, when memory suffices for touch—what it was like to walk out of my office, nonchalant and seemingly bored or distracted by demands. I would be nude beneath my proper grey skirt, keeping that particular secret like a card tucked away for a winning hand. (Not enough women wear stockings these days, and men seem to respond so well to that ridiculous bit of hosiery.) I'd duck into the conference room on the fifth floor and close the door against curious secretaries and clerks. And wait for you there, my heart beating a little faster as the heady world of business hummed around us. Then I'd hear you come in at last.

I remember feeling brash as I lifted up my skirt for the shock of showing off, becoming aroused before we'd even begun. Your eyes, quick kisses, then your hot mouth and clever tongue delving deep: I revelled in it. Your hands clutching my thighs, pulling me closer, famished for a woman. Stanley, believe me, I wasn't joking about the squirming, or the coming, either. It was so hard to keep quiet, but that added to the enjoyment, didn't it?

And then of course, I didn't mind turning around for you. I was always wet and more than happy to let you fuck me after I'd come, squirming against your insistent tongue. And you were always primed for me after a session with your head between my legs. I'd lean against the conference table, spreading my thighs, feeling like some model in a magazine. Playing the roles you men expect. Part of me liked that a lot, doing what those bimbos only act out. I played the slut well when I had to, something in me was excited as hell by it. It was about sex, but it was also about power...using it, buying it—and surrendering it. Who had the power? You or me?

I could speculate about that forever these days, lying back on my bed, hands cupping a breast, pouting for a suck, fingers wiggling into my slippery folds. Thinking about the illicit pleasures back then. You'd be almost panting behind me, unzipping yourself, hand on your cock, transformed into something primal. Pushing that warm erection into me, greed and haste burnishing everything. Urgency made it more exciting.

I could almost have loved you, Stanley. Almost.

I have needs, gentlemen, just like you. Appetites. But I never was a cartoon temptress. I was always discreet—except where bravado would be more effective—and I never was a threat to your wives. I didn't want what they had; I wanted something completely different from you. And I played fair, didn't I? I gave back as good as I got, both in what I gave and in the job I did.

Some of you don't like me, and that's all right. I didn't like all of you. And some of you didn't take what I offered. I respect that, and would never hold a polite *no, thank you* against you. And for some of you, I was just the wrong flavor. Who? Oh, no. That's their business, not yours.

So that's how I got here. I fucked my way up, enjoying a smorgasbord of men along the way. Greg in Accounting always did my reports first, and he gave me such good advice about where to cut the fat and where to prime the machine, that soon my division became stellar. That got noticed. I thanked him, of course. He loves blowjobs, and I don't mind them, either.

He'd groan *no*, but never actually try to stop me, gripping the armrests of his chair and grimacing as I teased him, crouching down, talking dirty until he was stiff. He was as appalled by us as he was delighted. I loved opening his belt, and getting it out, his flesh stiff with arousal, the man beneath the suit emerging, taking over. The carpeting in the office, I wasn't so crazy about, but I could get comfortable down there, closing my eyes beneath the fluorescents and imaging we were someplace else. I'd lick at his cock, rigid as the laws of numbers, sliding him in and out. If I said I didn't enjoy it, I'd be lying.

I'd take Greg over the edge, then leave him there, limp and satiated. I'd spend the rest of my day wanting more, the taste of his semen in my mouth. A secret.

Work and sex. Lucky for me, my career gave me both.

Of course, if I'd been nothing more than a good lay, I'd have gotten nowhere. But I had ambition and brains too, along with the body and appetite for pleasure. It's a lucky combination, and it's served me well. I may have slept my way up the corporate ladder and into my titles, but I know damned well that ability kept me there. Sex just helped slide things along more smoothly. Getting to know my colleagues—and superiors—a little better. To make sure they would remember me.

Eventually I reached VP of Production, reporting directly to the company President and no one else. The day Griffith Morgeson announced my assumption of the title, I sat in the boardroom, eyes directed modestly down on the walnut table, losing myself in the reflections on the surface. Idle thoughts occupied me while middle-aged voices droned on. Like other days when I got an edge by being a little whorish, I wore no panties under my silk suit, and desire, my silent partner, distracted me.

I waited, crossing and uncrossing my legs, until I thought I'd just have to slip my hand down there and rub all around until I came. I wanted to thank him—Griff—for the promotion in a very special way. How would I do it? Naked, in his office? My bare skin would be sweetly pink against his elegant upholstery. How could he say no? Surrounded by the unceasing momentum of commerce and propriety, the immediacy of lust would be even richer. I knew that well enough.

Or right there on the boardroom table? I squeezed my thighs together, cradling my want like a cupped flame in a storm. The table. I wanted to spread myself out, stripped of all my clothes, and share my success with everyone. Wouldn't that have been a fun way to make a Thursday meeting memorable? I couldn't, of course, but I fantasized about it for weeks afterward. The idea kept me wet for days: imagining a dozen scenarios with me brazen and naked on that hefty slab of corporate wood.

Each of you, taking a turn. Can you imagine that? I could. I liked the sex. And I liked the attention.

I know what it's like to feel your eyes on me, like a hundred softly whispered compliments, even as you listen to me talk about merges and strategy, staffing and consolidation. I relish the covert glance up from the report I've distributed, hungry on my breasts, hips, and ass. I don't blame you. You wonder if my nipples are neat, or big and bold, if I shave away the curls between my legs. Are my tits as nice out of my bra as they look in this sweater? I arch my back a little. I'm not above using what I've got to keep your attention. And yes—they are.

I imagine your daydreams. You've told me the nature of such things, decoded masculine speculation in post-coital confession. What would my ass feel like cupped in your hands as you slide my skirt up, your cock hard, excited ever more by the forbidden? Transgression is exciting. You watch me talk, and wonder what my mouth would look like circling you, engorged, on the cusp of release. It would look exciting, but it would feel even better. I know how to use my tongue.

You've heard whisper of rumors, shadows of words, all about me, and it intrigues you. You wonder if they're true. Domesticity is dull. So is this meeting. You imagine sliding your cock right into the velvet grip of me. Clench like a fist.

I behave impeccably, act the professional, tilting toward prim. Desire is pointless. There is no chance.

Then I give you a smile and you feel like it's your birthday.

Eventually, I fucked my way to the President. Ascending. Because power is sexy: wielding it, and being in its presence. I liked it, liked that scent of power like a whiff of high voltage, a heady thrum of something you can't quite see but can't help feel.

Griff was a widower, and a fairly nice guy. He was vigorous for his years, healthy and active, and I liked him. Company president, chief of staff. He had charm, rugged good looks, and outdoorsman's vitality, despite being a corporate executive, trapped in a world of desks and long lunches. He worked out regularly, and more women than me considered him attractive. Power suited him. A nice guy? By then, maybe, competition and determination worked out of his system (along with most, but not all, of his wild oats). He'd been mellowed by age, success, time and the first grandchild.

I was still hungry, though.

Hungry enough that when we took a meeting, I held his eyes too long. I smiled. I let my skirt rise like his hopes, and I left my blouse open to possibility. He wasn't stupid, and he could have had any woman he chose. I was attracted to him, and let him know it. *Choose me*, I willed. I'd make it so. I packaged my charms discreetly, and presented them quietly. The obvious tricks I'd used on some of you wouldn't work on him. But I knew with me, it would be different, and maybe he did, too. Almost a meeting of equals.

And he still had appetite for what I could offer: pleasure, along with a frisson of the forbidden. You know that combination. Guilt's a wonderful spice, just a pinch will do. Naughtiness is so very piquant.

One miserable afternoon in November, I decided the time was right to make my move. I asked to see Griff, alone, timing it for a quiet afternoon in a dull time of the year. I entered and sat in front of his desk, and he waited, tapping his pen. For the first time, I was nervous. This was the company president, after all. I'd never dared climb so high.

But I had prepared that morning, and it started the old sway of desire, like plucking a string and hearing it resonate long after.

It was dim in his office, the rain muting the day. Griff's desk lamp was on, casting a warm, intimate glow. I wanted to be in that golden circle of light. He'd shucked his jacket and rolled his shirtsleeves up. His arms were strong and muscular, still tanned. He'd been climbing mountains that autumn. He still wore his wedding ring, and I liked that touch of sentiment. Iron-grey hair brushed his forehead. He watched me look at him as the silence built between us. His strength—and his patience—were like granite. Solid. Grey. Griffith. His tie was dark red, a burgundy like spilled wine. Wine. I should have asked him out for a drink instead, done this over a glass or three in some dark and inviting place. But it was too late.

The silence lengthened and he, never a fool, waited, letting me be the first to speak. My heart was beating louder, I'd swear, and new nerves fluttered in my belly. One brow began to rise as the seconds built, and I wondered: under his white shirt, was his chest hairy? Of course it would be. I thought of brushing my breasts, nipples puckered and awaked, against that springy hair and the warmth of his skin. And just like that, I relaxed. I wanted him.

He finally spoke, filling the silence. "What can I do for you, Marianne?"

"You," I said, and stood.

Instinct took over. I hadn't really planned how I'd offer myself.

Then I knew: nude. Now.

I pretended that I knew what I was doing, and began to unbutton my blouse. Griff's hand went still, the pen resting in mid-tap. One button to three to them all, showing the lace I'd chosen. The blouse fell and his mouth opened.

I unzipped my skirt, let it drop, and got the bra off with minimum fumbling. My nipples hardened at my audacity. I'd either be fired or committed to the hospital downtown. But success—and prior experience—carried me through. Panties briefer than a winter day slid down my thighs. His eyes clouded, and I liked it.

I stripped in his office, slowly and completely, until I stood before his big desk, naked, completely nude. How did they describe the effects of an assault? Shock and awe? Yes, that's the effect it had on Griff, but in a nice way.

It excited me too. By the time that my panties slipped from one ankle, I was wet.

And he was hard.

I stood there, gift and reward, offering myself. He gave an inarticulate cry, and was around that desk faster than a nervous blink. For a minute, I thought he was going to run right past me and out of his office, barking for security. Doom. Then the lock clicked, and I knew he wanted it as much as I wanted to give it.

In seconds, Griff had me down on the floor, my knees up, and he straddled me, shaking his head. Bemusement, amusement, disbelief. And lust. I could see the hard-on in his grey trousers and it pleased me enormously. I couldn't wait to touch it. His skin would be hot against my tongue. The throb of him, caught up, like a leaf in a swollen spring river, in wanting.

Stripped of my corporate pretence, I was his. My skin warm against the carpet in his office. My nudity turned me to honey inside. Pinned beneath him, exactly where I wanted to be.

He knelt over me, conqueror, denying me the role of seductress, taking charge. Good. Then when he looked back, whatever happened would burn as a mutual event. I had provoked, but he seized the bait. Griff didn't speak, he just looked down at me, grey wool trousers trying to hold back the evidence of his arousal. I'd never felt more naked, more exposed in my life, but it was all right, I knew it. My nipples were hard—exhilaration, fear, or desire, or it may have been a combination of all those turbulent feelings flying through me. He touched my right nipple, as if considering what was offered to him, rolling it slowly with his thumb and finger. I moaned.

"Okay," he muttered. "Okay."

He unzipped his trousers, got his belt open, and his nakedness broke out to join mine. His cock thrust out, weighty and potent, just like the man. I eyed it, longing. I was all promise, entirely consent, and knew no foreplay was required. My undressing had been enough. For both of us.

In but a moment, he was between my legs, and he swallowed the nipple he'd touched, sucking hard, pushing his erection into me. His tie dangled down for a moment, then red silk was crushed in our coupling. My bare thighs slid along the fine weave of his trousers, and his cock made me whole. Held down on the office carpet with his body, with nothing to soften his thrusts, Griff took me. Fast, furious and hard, and he found me molten within.

I'd been ready all morning, ready for weeks, and slid up to meet each thrust, wetting him. He quickened, I hung on, climax as inevitable as sunrise. He sucked my nipple, frantic, then reared up, pounding into me, his face stripped of convention's mask, naked in his pleasure. His thrusts created my release. Like a figure on horseback emerging from a sandstorm, chaos coalesced, everything to a single thing: I was just about to... "Griff," I prayed, hoarse, the compulsion to tell. He fucked me. "I'm coming..."

His kiss silenced me, and I soared, biting his tongue, hot and wet.

He followed a second later, stifling his own cry into my hair. I tried, as always, to feel the moment the rush of semen began, but couldn't quite tell when the first erupted or the last ended. Only by his slowing thrusts, his ragged breath, his last shudder, did I know when his release had swept through him.

"What do you want?" he asked when we were done. I floated back to shore, aware of the carpet against my skin, the ceiling of Griff's office, the sound of business continuing beyond his door, our interlude. The phone had rung on his desk unanswered; soft knocks at the door were ignored. I pictured his secretary outside, fuming, and hoped she was discreet.

"Nothing," I replied, and maybe, just at that moment, that was even true.

We had an affair. It was almost the best time of my life. I had it all. I was fucking the boss and loving every minute of it. I never asked for more than he chose to give. I never pestered him to make a commitment, to spend the holidays with me, to buy me things. I didn't need him for that, and I liked my private time, too. I was still an executive with plenty of my own responsibilities and constant demands on my time. I liked his companionship and he was a fine partner in bed. If being on such good terms with the company president helped me in my career, then so be it. He got a lot of enjoyment out of our time together. I played fair.

I never asked for more than what he offered. And eventually, he offered a lot.

I'd fucked my way to the top floor, the penthouse suite of a glass-steel-and-more-glass building filled with egos as big as monuments, and I went right through that ceiling. On my knees, sure, or on my back, or at my desk, I didn't care which helped get me there.

He offered everything. Gold ring: that was my prize. I was indecisive for days. Then not. We were married.

And it was good. I knew there would be no children, and I knew he was used to living life on his terms. I knew I was stepping into a role another woman had originated, but I was nothing like his first wife, and even his children allowed him the consolation of a second marriage.

Then, as you know, Griff died. Heart attack, at the summer place. And yes, the rumors about that are true, too. He went out with a smile on his face, because he'd just finished fucking me. It had been a bit more enthusiastic than usual, and he'd rolled over at the end, complaining about being exhausted. Smug, I thought I'd worn him out. He stepped away for a cigar on the deck at sunset. And that's where he went.

Funny, he didn't call for me, or try to save himself. He died well, I think. He didn't linger; he didn't become pathetic.

And he was where he wanted to be, although at his desk would have been just as likely, considering Griff had a hard time letting go of anything that he'd worked hard to get.

So he was gone. And I found that I missed him far more than I'd expected to. I missed that son-of-a-bitch a lot. I thought it had all been about opportunity and bargains, about doing what I had to do. Then why did it hurt so much to be without him? And my body craved what he'd been giving me regularly—that vigor was expressed in more places than the boardroom and the golf course—I missed that, too.

I still wanted to fuck but now I also wanted to wake up in the morning and find the same person on the other pillow day after day. Griff. That I wanted a person on the other pillow surprised me. I haven't been that sentimental in years, but I got used to having someone...around.

And the thing of it is? Almost any one of you guys would be happy to step up and fill the President's shoes—and his bed. But I don't want you any more. And there's nowhere to go, now.

Anyway. I know it's an unusual resignation, but there you go, boys. Cream in your Armanis, jump in your handmade shoes. Someone younger and hungrier can take my place now. I did get what I'd wanted, and I left my mark. Money? You always ask about money. Well, I've got enough of that for the rest of my days. I don't care.

Work? My heart's not in it any more. It's time to retire.

It's lonely at the top.

TOUCH
by Rachel Kramer Bussel
for Kristin

"Most profoundly, it [sex] is an act of opening
up to one another. It is a sharing of energies. It
doesn't ask you to be a certain way. It shows
you how you are."
—David Guy, *The Red Thread of Passion:
Spirituality and the Paradox of Sex*

While I'm inside of her, the world stops and nothing else
matters. We are the only people who exist, now, or ever. I
lose myself as my hands roam along her pale skin, and am
completely gone once they reach between her legs, where
she is always wet and more than ready. Even for me,
sometimes the most talkative girl in the world, there are times
that words fail me, and this is one of them. I have very little
to say as I spread her open, as I reach literally inside of her,
and even though I've done it many times before and will do
so many times again, each time I touch her, it's different, awe-
inspiring and amazing. Each time it's almost a surprise to
find her so eager, so wet she is almost dripping and my
fingers slide into her as if they were made to fuck her. Each
time, it's almost like a miracle, and in that instant that I enter
her, all my doubts and worries slip away and my life is only
about this simple, yet profound, touch.

I approach her always with the best of intentions, to expand my horizons, to utilize the vast array of sex toys lying on all sides of me, but tonight, like most nights, I don't really want any of them. My eyes glance over them and then back to the beauty of her cunt, beckoning to me. I want, actually I need, to feel her for myself as my fingers coax their way down her body, brushing over her cheek, pressing into her neck, sliding down her chest to dawdle at her nipples, then curving around her hip as my tongue dances its way along her slightly curved stomach. There is so much of her I could linger on, and feeling her impatience only makes me want to prolong things until I touch her where she most wants me to, knowing she will be all the more ready for me when I get there. I lick along the fine skin of her stomach, press my cheek against this softest of flesh until even I can no longer stand the wait. My attempts to tease her have left me on edge, too.

Sometimes I watch, looking down as my fingers slip inside her, as she pulls them deeper and sucks me into her. Other times I lie alongside her and whisper into her ear, tell her what it feels like as I slam my way into her, rough and then gentle, gentle and then rough. Though I spend most of the day apart from her thinking about this very moment, once it arrives I have no plan or map to guide me, only the way she rocks against me and gives me invaluable clues in the art of pleasing her.

Time stops, stands still, turns around, remakes itself as we remake ourselves. I have no time to think or process, only the present, to go by instinct as I lose myself inside of her. I shift around, trying to find the most comfortable spot, the place that allows me to touch the most of her skin, not just inside but out, where I can feel her warmth and breath and presence. I like to lie lengthwise against her so I can simultaneously touch her head, arm, chest, side, and legs, all the while plunging my fingers inside her. The best part, or one of many best parts about it, is hearing her breath in my ear, a quiet, intimate noise that I miss when my head is not directly next to hers. Through her breathing, almost more than the wetness surrounding my fingers, I can tell when she is getting closer, getting more away from her normal, everyday self and into that place that we go to alone, together. I live for those moments when I can make her lose control, when the only thing that matters is me pressing into her and her pressing back against me, when the only thing left for her to do is take ragged breaths that seem to catch on themselves, to claw at me in desperation, to bite my arm to show me how much she likes what I'm doing. I want to stay like that forever, even more than I want to make her come, to feel her hot breath on me and sink inside her, towards salvation.

I'm not exactly a religious person, though there have been times when I've moved more in that direction. I'm always plagued with too many doubts, logical twists that prevent me from taking that full leap into faith.

And yet that's exactly how it is, with that same intangible faith that true prayer and worship requires, I seek her out, find new ways to fill up the empty spaces inside of her, new ways to make her squeeze my hand until I think it will break. I didn't realize until recently how powerful that connection was, perhaps because I have always had trouble with the concept of faith, logician that I am. I was always the one asking "why?" and "how?"—needing proof instead of long-passed-on fables, needing times and dates and names and places to make real for me the strength of a miracle. But with her I feel like anything is possible; if I can make her body sing in this way, can bring us both to somewhere we've never been before, over and over again, is that not its own miracle?

I've been the same way about love, not believing that one person could truly do it all for me, that sex could be a communion of sorts rather than a physical act. With her, it's like sex as I knew it, used to think I knew it, used to think I had a remote clue about what it was, falls away and we are reinventing it, and ourselves, over and over again. Sometimes we spend so many minutes, hours, days lost in our own cocoon, lost in each other's bodies, that I can't function once I leave her, don't know what to do in the "real world" because she is the only thing that's real to me anymore.

The boys on TV ask me how they should touch a woman, seeking some magic formula that will make them the perfect lovers, bring their girlfriends to sure-fire orgasms, but the truth is I have no idea. When I'm with her I'm no longer any kind of expert, I barely even know my name except when she says it, all deep and throaty and needy. Most of the time I don't know what I'm doing, don't know where I'm touching her, don't have a technical name for it or a recalled memory of reading or writing about this. I couldn't, because I've never felt or done anything like this before. With her, I'm not a sexpert but a sorcerer, a magician feeling my way along, teasing, testing, probing, hoping.

Every time I touch her, I do so by instinct, and if I were to stop and think about it I'd be wracked by insecurity, yet with her it all makes perfect sense. She used to say to me, in that breathy, high-on-sex kind of way, "you know exactly how to touch me," and I thought it wasn't true, or an exaggeration. I didn't feel like I knew; it was maybe a happy accident, but maybe my body knew before I did, instinctively. At first I wasn't sure what to do with her, what to do with this sensual, beautiful woman with the body of a girl, all slim and thin and seemingly fragile. I didn't know that I could put as many fingers as I want inside of her, and she'd eagerly claim them, didn't know that instead of being fragile she is infinitely strong; in fact, it's a challenge to break her, to make her shake and shiver and moan, to give up some of that strength to me.

I didn't know that sliding my fingers inside of her, something as seemingly simple as that, could bring tears to my eyes, could make me want to stay there forever. I didn't know that being the one doing the fucking could bring me to the same heights as being the one getting fucked, could make me feel so free and high and happy.

A snapshot: She is lying across the queen size bed, her head hanging off the side of it, spread out before me like the most delicious buffet. I have been away for a weekend that feels like much longer, and I look at her and it's almost like I've never seen her before. I am nervous and ravenous at the same time, and watching my fingers move over and around her hot pink lips, I shiver, unsure whether to try to control myself or to let myself go. As I slide my fingers into her, first one and then two, and then more, until I have most of one hand pressed deeply inside of her, I marvel at the way she feels. I am touching skin and heat and pressing up against bones and flesh and she asks me what I'm doing to her, and I kiss her instead because I don't have an answer for her. She is more mysterious than any boy will ever be, holding so many more secrets inside of her, ones I live to unearth.

I love that I can bring her so much pleasure by simply turning my wrist this way and that, minute movements that rock her body until I can't stand it anymore and just press as deeply as I can. I am pushing and straining and wondering when she will tell me to stop when she says "More, deeper" and grabs my wrist and pushes it towards her in a moment of frantic desperation. She lets go, only to claw at me, clutch at me for support lest she fall too far away from this world. I again push my four fingers deep inside and marvel that she can take so much. I push and twist and strain, my own breathing heavy as I sweat while I push, sometimes shaking my whole body back and forth, rocking slightly in unison with her. Even though I'm pressing against her from the inside out, it feels the opposite. I feel like I am pulling her to me, holding onto her from the outside in, taking from her ever so much more than giving to her, trying to make sure, even though I know it is impossible, that she will be right here, mine, forever.

With eyes closed and breath frantic, she whispers words that enter my soul, that stay with me, haunting me late at night as my mind repeats them and my body reacts involuntarily. She tells me secrets and needs and dreams, saying words I don't think I want to hear until they sound so right as they escape her. She tells me I can do whatever I want to her, and suddenly what I want to do to her expands, racing from simple wishes to a need to consume and devour. An indescribable emotion, something like pride, or lust, or greed, one of those deadly sins we are not supposed to feel, bubbles up, as she lets me touch her everywhere, lets me take us both into uncharted territory. I scare myself a little as her words pump into me, druglike. My reaction is not what I would have predicted, but nothing about us is what I would have expected.

She is so beautiful, I want to climb inside her, live forever inside her beauty as she continues to open and open and open for me. She makes me want to put my entire self into her, to give her all of me and see what she can do with it, to keep her here, ready and open just for me, always. Every time she does so I am in awe of her, of how she can tear me up and twist me around and make me lose myself inside of her, of how she makes the art of getting fucked one that requires true passion and discipline and devotion. She is not the kind of girl who ever lies there and takes it, but one who wrestles with me, verbally and physically, challenging me to push her to new heights, to test my own boundaries, to go deeper, literally and figuratively. I hold one hip and with my fingers inside of her rock her whole body, gently at first and then more firmly, watching her breasts jiggle like a doll as her cunt tightens around me.

She sucks me into her, literally and figuratively, drawing me closer and closer until it would be impossible to turn away even if I wanted to. My thumb massaging her clit makes her spasm involuntarily, pulling me in deeper, and I know she wants more. I look up at her face, want to see her eyes before I enter her further, but they are firmly shut and I close my own for a minute and then slide my other hand inside, palms pressed together as if in prayer. And this is truly a form of prayer, a form of worship of something that is not altogether of this world. Our love, our meeting, our understanding of each other is not something that was planned in any way and yet it now seems fated. I move my hands slowly, sliding them back and forth, gently coaxing her orgasm from wherever it is lurking. I lean my head against her stomach, as if to feel and hear and sense what's happening inside. When it happens, it's like an earthquake, not an 8, but a gently building 3, roiling and tumbling as it gathers steam until it finally erupts, lingering far longer than it has any right to.

Even when I slide my hands out of her, as slowly as I can and with great reluctance, I can feel her trembling underneath me, our connection not severed by the lack of physical contact in that most intimate of places. I pull her towards me and listen to the final shudders that wrack her, and then I pull her closer and I can feel tears fill my eyes. There are no words left for this moment, no way to show or tell her how she can undo me with her trembling, how she intoxicates me. I'm torn between holding her in my arms and kissing her gently and throwing her back down on the bed, face down this time, and plunging back into her.

After, I can't stop feeling like a part of me is still with her. For days afterwards, my hands are no longer simply my hands; they are beautiful, magical, and all I want to do with them is touch her again, and again. The way it feels to be inside of her lingers as I type at my keyboard or load my papers into the copier at work, and I marvel that these same hands can perform such mundane tasks alongside such amazing feats. They feel bigger, stronger, as do I.

Our desire for each other is like an endless cycle, and just when I think I've perhaps had enough, am ready to sleep or simply to hold her, she presses against me in a certain way, darts her tongue out to lick my ear or tells me something so fabulously dirty I can think only of having her yet again. When we are naked like this, pressed against each other after we've spent all day in bed, life is as perfect as it will ever get.

I never thought the point of religion was to absolve all my sins or answer all my questions, yet I felt cheated when my questions could not be answered, the options too intangible for me to fathom. And yet somehow she manages to answer the questions I haven't even asked, and without even meaning to makes me whole and alive. Naked, she is like my angel, my peace offering, everything I will ever need to get by.

When I'm with her, the world stops and nothing else matters. We are the only people who exist, now, or ever. She is my savior, my treasure, my angel. She is the answer to all my prayers, especially the ones I never even knew I had.

BARELY CONNECTING
by Lacey Savage

He still hadn't called.

Seven days, fourteen hours, thirty-three minutes and counting, and not a word from Jenson. Telling your girlfriend of four years that you think you've been "missing out on dating experiences" should warrant at least a phone call a few days later. Just to check in, to say hello, or maybe even to inquire as to the state of said girlfriend's crushed heart.

But no, that wasn't Jenson's style. He'd expect her to come crawling back, in tears, black mascara streaking down her cheeks giving her the sexy look of a raccoon. He'd want her to throw herself at his feet, perhaps dressed in a long trench coat and nothing else. She'd unbutton the loose garment and entice him with her body, shoving her plump, firm breasts forward, promising a myriad of sexual experiences to make up for those dating ones he yearned for.

Well, he'd better be prepared to wait a long time.

Christa stretched her long legs out in front of her and got up from the desk. A thick, gray cloud cover obstructed the sun outside the forty-second story window, and heavy raindrops suddenly filled the air. Christa watched the fat drops splatter against the windowpane, and she caught her reflection in the glass. Her lower lip stuck out slightly and her small mouth was turned downward in a pout.

Jenson loved to nibble on that lip while he fucked her.

She grasped her lower lip gently between her teeth and closed her eyes, leaning her forehead on the cold windowpane. She could feel the weight of Jenson's body on top of hers, the strong muscles in his arms as she held on for dear life while he thrust his cock in and out of her body, the ripples in his abs contracting tightly with every move. She remembered the way they'd sprawl there afterwards, limbs entangled, the smell of sweat and sex permeating the room.

The sound of someone clearing his throat startled her out of her reverie.

"I have a delivery for Miss Brooks." The tall man hunched slightly forward while he stood in the doorway. One arm hung limply at his side, the sleeve of his jacket ending closer to his elbow than his wrist. In his other hand, he held a long box tied with a red ribbon.

"I'm Christa Brooks." She reached into her pocket and handed him a dollar, then took the box he held out to her. She set the container on her desk and stared at it for a full minute, working up the courage to open it. Jenson never did things like this. It couldn't possibly be a gift from him... could it?

She leaned over and pulled off the lid in one swift move. Inside the plain cardboard container lay a single red rose. The card attached read simply,

The Seven Hearts Motel
6:00 P.M.
Room 215

J.

Well, damn. Christa stared at Jenson's messy handwriting, running a finger over the crooked loop of the letter J. He wanted to see her. At a motel, of all places! He must be horny... a week is a long time to go without when you're used to having it daily.

She put the rose back in the box and replaced the lid. Picking up her keys from the desk, she grabbed the container and with a quick glance at the clock, hurried across the hallway to the elevator. She had an hour and a half to go home and change before meeting Jenson at the motel. Christa's pulse quickened at the thought of his mouth ravaging every inch of her body, ripping off her clothes, pinning her to the mattress… okay, so *one* of them was horny, at any rate. She groaned as the elevator doors closed, sealing her inside with her lust-filled thoughts.

Her digital watch read a little after six when she pulled into a parking space outside the main doors to The Seven Hearts Motel. The parking lot was well lit by the large neon sign announcing the going hourly rate. So much for class. But then again, she hadn't expected the Ritz. Not from Jenson. The man didn't have a romantic bone in his body.

And why was she here, anyway? She should have been angry. Livid, even! And instead, the only thing she could think about was storming into that motel room and undressing. Being naked—gloriously naked, allowing for nothing but that skin on skin contact she craved. There would be no secrets between them when the clothes were shed. No "missed experiences." Only the bare naked truth.

The door to room 215 badly needed a fresh coat of paint. Flakes of the dirty white coating came loose and fell on the shaggy brown carpet as Christa knocked tentatively. The sound of the lock turning followed a short silence, during which Christa took the opportunity to hike her short skirt up a little higher. The sounds of the jungle assaulted her ears when Jenson pulled the door open. He stood there, grinning, his eyes wide with surprise as he looked her over.

"Were you expecting someone else?" she asked.

"My girlfriend," Jenson said, stepping out of the way to

allow her to enter the room. "She's about your height, blonde hair, green eyes… well, she looks a lot like you, but I've never seen her wear anything even resembling *that*."

Christa spun around slowly, allowing him a better look. She'd carefully chosen the tight, black miniskirt and red low-cut tank top. She feared her breasts would fall out at any moment and already the tip of a dark nipple eagerly peeked over the constraints of the fabric. Black sheer stockings and thigh-high, fuck-me boots completed the ensemble, and her hair fell loose around her shoulders—mostly due to the fact that she had been running late than any conscious attempt at a sultry, windswept look.

"What is that sound?" she asked, as a particularly high-pitched bird call resonated from the small stereo system on the table.

"It was all they had," he shrugged apologetically. "It goes with the ambiance, I guess."

Jenson flicked off the light switch, and the room became bathed in a golden glow. Christa suddenly became aware of the candles that covered every surface. The room was as wild as the music, tackily decorated in leopard print and jungle décor, but the candlelight managed to give it a soft, almost romantic glow.

"We need to talk," she said, spinning around quickly to face him. Jenson stood in the middle of the room, unbuttoning his shirt. He'd already tossed his jeans on the back of a nearby chair. She watched him pull off his gray briefs and throw them over the jeans. His cock stood out, thick and hard among a sea of black curls.

"Don't you think we should—"

Her words were cut off as Jenson closed the space between them. His mouth clamped on top of hers, his tongue thrusting its way between her lips. He ran his teeth lightly over her lower lip and she moaned, closing her eyes and pressing her breasts against his chest. She could feel her juices start to run down her thighs, and she moaned against his wet mouth. Not wearing panties had its advantages.

Christa's hands roamed over Jenson's naked shoulders, gripping him tightly and pulling him in to deepen the kiss. She continued to explore his body, running her palms over his back and bringing them lower to cup his ass in her hands. When her fingers ran lightly across his cock, Jenson inhaled sharply and pulled back.

"No," he said, backing away a few steps as if afraid to have her touch him.

"No?" Christa echoed, surprised by the sudden turn of events. "You don't want me?"

"Oh, I want you. But this is your night. Take off your clothes and lie on the bed. Face-down."

Christa nodded, too aroused to question him. She pulled the tight top over her head quickly and tossed it on the floor. Her breasts, suddenly free from the tight fabric, bounced slightly as she unzipped her skirt and let it fall to the ground beside her blouse. She heard Jenson's intake of breath as he noticed the absence of panties underneath the short skirt. The boots came off next, followed by the black stockings.

Keenly aware of Jenson's eyes on her body, Christa moved to the bed and stretched out on the leopard-print covers. She rested her head on her arms and waited expectantly for his next move.

Jenson approached the bed, holding a bowl in his hands. Christa could see a red plastic bottle jutting out from it. After setting the bowl down on the nightstand, Jenson picked up the bottle and removed the cap. Christa lost sight of her man for a moment while he moved behind her.

The bed squeaked when Jenson climbed up on it, and Christa felt him swing a leg over her body and straddle her, sitting on the back of her legs. She sighed contentedly when she felt his cock nudge the curve of her ass.

"Fuck me," she whispered. Her swollen lips throbbed almost painfully. She pressed herself deeper into the leopard-print comforter, lifting her hips, prodding his cock with her ass.

The sharp sting of his slap was unexpected, and Christa groaned, burying her face in the pillow as another blow landed on her left cheek. She loved being spanked, and the bastard knew it! Each sting felt heavenly, the pain mixing with her need to be fucked, and bringing her to the edge before merging abruptly with the delicious agony of another slap.

She felt her moist liquid heat run freely between her legs and onto the covers beneath her body. Christa panted, trying to hold back her moans as his hand fell closer and closer to the slit of her cunt. She lifted herself up on her knees, giving him greater access to her ass and the space between her legs. He continued to spank her, rhythmically, open-handed, the sound of his palm connecting with her bare skin filling the room. Using his other hand, he plunged two fingers inside her, and Christa knew she teetered on the edge of losing control. Her ass tingled with the pain of the blows, and her pussy clamped down on Jenson's fingers. She bit into the pillow to keep from screaming as her body trembled with the powerful orgasm. She was vaguely aware of the sound of an elephant trumpeting accompanying her muffled cries.

When he stopped spanking her, she waited for the overwhelming rush to subside. Jenson positioned himself back on top of her legs, holding her pinned to the bed. She tried to lift her head, but couldn't see what he held in his hand. A warm, silky liquid flowed over the right cheek of her ass, caressing the spot he had slapped just moments before. Jenson's palm took on a gentle touch as he let his hand glide over her ass, rubbing the oil into her skin.

Christa sighed, letting herself relax. His hands continued to caress her ass moving up languidly over her back in long, even strokes. The smell of strawberries drifted up from the oil, and she inhaled deeply, savoring the feeling of his strong hands on her bare skin.

"That feels incredible," she whispered as Jenson's hand slid between her pussy lips. The massage oil and the wetness of her pussy coated his fingers, and they glided inside her easily. She lifted her hips, encouraging him to plunge deeper, but he removed his fingers and continued massaging her back. He ran his palms along the sides of her body, pushing up toward her shoulder blades, and then lessening the pressure and coming back down to her ass.

The sensual massage had aroused her, and she could feel her pussy throbbing slightly. When Jenson lifted himself off her, Christa felt empty, as if a part of her went with him. She whimpered in protest.

"Turn over." His fingers gently nudged her onto her back.

She stared into his brown eyes and smiled. Jenson reached for the oil. She watched him pour the velvety liquid onto her breasts and over her flat stomach. Where his hands connected with her bare skin, she shivered under his touch. His expert palms caressed her breasts, his fingers kneading the heavy globes as he spread the strawberry oil on her tan skin and over the taut nipples. He moved to her belly, arms, and legs, running his hands down to the top of her feet, slipping a wet finger between her toes. She wriggled on the bed, relishing the slightly ticklish sensation.

Oil covered Christa's body, which shone in the candlelight from the slick and sticky liquid. She could smell her arousal mixed with the fruity scent of the massage oil, and she sighed deeply, spreading her legs wider apart.

Finished with her feet, Jenson rose from the bed and stood over her. His cock looked rock hard, and Christa wondered absentmindedly if it had stayed that way the entire massage. She had managed to lose track of time, lost in the blissful and hypnotic feel of his hands.

"Am I forgiven?" he asked, his gaze piercing into hers, his jaw clenched as if expecting her to say "no."

She couldn't disappoint. "No."

His eyebrows lifted in surprise. "No?"

"Not yet," she replied. She ran her tongue over her upper lip, then motioned to the bottle on the nightstand. "That stuff's edible, I assume?"

A grin spread slowly over his features as he climbed back onto bed and positioned himself between her legs. Lowering his head, Jenson flicked his tongue tentatively between the lips of her pussy, then delved deeper inside. Christa moaned, her head thrashing from side to side while his tongue continued its merciless taunting. She lifted her hips off the bed and her legs stiffened as she entangled her fingers in Jenson's hair and pulled him closer to her. When she felt him suck her swollen clit between his lips, Christa couldn't hold the climax back any longer. It set her body on fire, her breath coming in quick spurts as Jenson's tongue lapped mercilessly at the wetness that flowed freely from her cunt.

Christa kept her eyes closed, and became briefly aware of Jenson detaching himself from her pussy and moving up beside her. She felt his fingers lightly pinch her nipple, and she opened her eyes to stare into his. He hadn't bothered to wipe her juices off his face, and his chin glistened. Christa flicked her tongue over the cleft in his square jaw, tasting herself on him.

"So this is your answer to everything?" she asked, running her manicured fingernails over his smooth chest.

"Not everything," he replied. "Just the important things."

Jenson's mouth met hers. The kiss felt possessive, his need to lay claim to her broadcast through his probing tongue.

"I'll take you to Paris," she said when he broke away.

His thick brows drew together, shadowing his eyes. "Why?"

"You want a variety of dating experiences. We've never dated in Paris."

"But we've fucked in the jungle," he said, straight-faced, indicating the room around them. The wild call of birds, and the occasional howl of a wild animal accompanied Christa's torrential giggles.

THE ART OF EXPOSURE
by Tenille Brown

It lay exquisite, perfect and round. Like a caramel-tipped hill against a smooth endless sky, it sat motionless. It was the most magnificent piece he had observed all evening, and it held him captive.

He wondered if he should speak on it, compliment its grace and the simplicity of which it was displayed, but he knew that if he spoke even one word, or merely kept looking at it this way, it could vanish as quickly as it had appeared.

So, he just stared. He stared so hard and so long that she lifted her eyes from the miniature statue she had been admiring and smiled. He smiled back hoping she would be none the wiser, but the sudden breeze that rushed through the room and the uncomfortable grunt of the woman standing next to her deemed it necessary for her to glance down at her bosom.

And in a hurried sweep, it was gone.

She adjusted the scoop of her neckline to cover her stray breast. She brought her hand to her mouth in mock embarrassment and narrowed her eyes. "I'm sorry," she said. "I didn't mean to flash you."

He wanted to thank her for it, actually, but said instead, "It's quite all right. I hardly noticed."

Strikingly high heels put her at eye level with him. Her hair was swept into a long honey ponytail that rested on a shoulder the color of ginger. Her brown eyes were wide and bright, her lips full and glossed. And though her slinky brown dress remained intact, he noted that the rest of her was equally exceptional. But his eyes fell again to her chest, now hidden behind her tightly folded arms.

Anxious to fill the uncomfortable silence that stretched between them, he extended his hand. "Gil."

She accepted his hand, not shaking or even grasping it, merely touching it gently. "Julia," she said, then pointing toward her breast, "and you've already been introduced to my tit."

"Yes, I believe so," Gil laughed, then shuffled his feet.

For the brief moment she left her arms at her sides, his eyes found their way there again, to that glorious, smooth space between her full cleavage. He watched the silk dress caress her skin and he willed it to fall out of sorts once more, for just a moment so that he could experience the bliss of her beautiful breast once more.

"It's amazing isn't it?"

Gil's eyes snapped to attention as Julia pointed to the statue.

"Yes, lovely." But he was thinking on another thing, the thing that truly was amazing, the thing had caught the fast attention of his groin. "Are you thinking of buying it?"

Julia cocked her head. "I don't know. I'm not so sure how well it would fit in my house."

"Do you live near here?" If she did, he wanted to know where. He wanted to drive slowly through her neighborhood and watch her walk to her mailbox. He wanted to stand outside her window at bedtime, wanted to watch her step in and out of the shower.

"Yes, for a bit. But my husband just bought a house in Paris. I've acquired three pieces for it already."

There was a husband. Strangely, this disappointed him, but before he had time to curse the gods for not bringing this woman to him sooner, before there was the liability of marriage, the sudden feel of a familiar hand sliding around his waist reminded him that there was also a wife.

"See anything you like?" Linda was restless, playing with the strand of pearls that clung tight to her neck.

Gil patted her hand. "As a matter of fact, I do. But I want to think about it a while before I make an offer."

He gently squeezed Linda's shoulder, and as he guided her away from the small crowd of patrons, he felt a tug at his elbow. He turned as Julia pressed a card into his palm, her fingers lingering long enough to cause a tingle in his thighs and tightness in his chest.

"If you'd ever like to make an offer," she said.

Gil forced his eyes away as Julia became lost in the crowd of tailored suits and designer gowns. He pretended not to notice Linda taking in his discomfort.

"She's an artist," Gil explained to Linda's questioning glance. "She has a piece I'd like to take a look at."

Linda nodded, satisfied, and he led her in the opposite direction, pushing the memory of a well- proportioned and fully exposed breast to the back of his mind.

The rain made music on her roof. Julia sat close to Gil on the couch in dark slacks and a white blouse with three buttons undone. He watched the shirt rise and hug her breasts as she lifted her arms high in a silent yawn. He watched it fall open just a little more as she let her hands drop to her knees.

"I'm sorry to just call you up like that, but I was doing business near here and thought I might pop in and see what you've got." It sounded reasonable enough. After all he had suffered through four days of constant recollections and unimaginable restraint. And the truth was, he was hoping to catch her not so done up, maybe half-dressed or even undressed, awakening from an afternoon nap or preparing for a bath.

She smiled that painfully delicious smile. "It's fine, Gil. Actually, I thought you would have called days ago." Julia tucked one bare foot beneath her, her knee pressed against his thigh.

"Well I wanted to give you a little time, you know, to get things in order. I didn't know how you go about showing your work."

She nudged his thigh with her knee and winked. Her heat bore into him. He ventured to touch her hand.

Her cleavage pressed against the opening of her blouse and he wondered if she was bare underneath, if all that kept him from his long awaited bliss was the thin veil of her top. He shifted ever so carefully to adjust his trousers to accommodate the growing discomfort in his shorts.

She leaned forward then, lifting her iced brandy from the coffee table and bringing it to her lips. As she did this, one glorious breast came forth as if called, the smooth nipple resting erect. It sat there so simple, yet so inviting that his hand moved forward and touched it gently.

He watched her eyes, ready to pull his hand away and tuck it in his pocket where it would behave, ready to reach for her other breast and kiss and caress both until she moaned.

And she did moan.

She freed her hands of her drink and reached for him. She brushed her fingers across his cheek, then brought his head gently forward, nuzzling his face there. She guided his hands to the buttons and he undid them all and pushed the blouse off her shoulders. He stood up and extended his hand to her, pulling her up in front of him. His lips and tongue ached for the taste of her skin, but he longed to see all of her first. He unbuttoned and unzipped her slacks, pushed them down to her thighs and she lifted each leg high until they fell to her ankles and she stepped out of them and pushed them out of the way.

Her sheer panties hinted of a luscious cunt covered with a fine layer of hair. She removed the panties as well, and finally undone, she stood exposed, the whole of her. He drank in her golden perfection as she tussled her hair.

He stood dangerously close to her nakedness, and his own shirt and tie began to choke him. As if sensing his need to escape his own binding, Julia undid his tie and pulled it from around his neck. In hurried movements she undid the buttons of his shirt and the latch of his trousers. She caressed his cock through his boxers and rid him of those as well.

They stood, exposed and without the burden of clothes.

Gil circled her, studied the curves in her breasts and hips, the flatness of her tummy, the slightly darker circles that were her elbows and knees. His cock extended before him like a smooth dark sword and, nearing her again, it brushed her thigh. Julia placed her hands on his waist and pulled him toward her. Bringing her face to his, her tongue found his. Intoxicated on the taste of her, he staggered and lowered himself on the couch. Immediately, she knelt between his knees. Taking the whole of him in her mouth, she moved up and down, her eyes never leaving his.

His hands rested on her neck, roamed her shoulders and back. He ran his fingers through her hair. When he could take no more, he pulled her onto his lap where she settled comfortably for a slow ride down his cock.

The inside of her was warm and soft; the grip of her cunt on his cock was strong and mesmerizing. Julia moved on his cock with the beauty and preciseness of a ballerina. Her thighs caressed his, her knees pressed into his ass. He buried his head beneath her chin, cupped her breasts in both hands. He brought one perfect brown nipple to his lips. Gil's tongue traveled the roundness of it, tasted the sweetness of it. He held the other between his fingers and rubbed until he evoked a harsh sigh from her lips.

His hands found her waist again and he maneuvered her onto her back and hovered over her. Distracting her with his tongue in her mouth, he pushed into her gently, yet urgently and closed his eyes against the pleasure. He buried his head in her hair, inhaling her sweetness as he pushed and pulled, then slipped into the ecstasy of release.

Julia's forehead rested on his shoulder. Her hair was wet against his back. She lifted her head and kissed his cheek, her breasts still pressed against his chest. "I can try to have that piece ready for you by the weekend. Do you think you can come back then?"

He thought he could come back. He thought he could come back again and again. Unable to find his voice, Gil nodded and when his breathing quieted, he heard the rain again.

Gil guessed it had taken her a few hours at most. He looked from a distance, twisted and turned to see it from all angles. The pattern was irregular and exotic, the colors wild and bright. Every spot was attended to, every curve, every mound. He nodded his approval at her work and she stood content to have pleased him.

"You can touch, you know."

And as if permission was what he was waiting for, he touched where there was purple, rubbed where there was red, caressed where there was blue.

She was marvelous.

"It's beautiful, Julia," he said, as if words were enough. "But would you mind terribly if I ruined it now?"

She shrugged. "I suppose not. It's yours after all."

He took her by her hand, led her through her bedroom to the shower. In the bathroom mirror he admired it once more, the abstract masterpiece that covered her from her forehead to her toes. The paint was almost as maddening as clothes and he was frantic to get it off her skin.

Leaving his trousers and shirt in a heap, Gil stepped into the warm burst of water. He pulled Julia in, positioning her in front of him so that the water sprayed against her back, soaked her hair and ran down her face.

Gil rubbed the loosening paint from her body, the yellow from her breasts, the green from her belly and cunt. His own body tucked into hers, his cock rose against her thigh and as the colors streamed down her arms and legs, he kissed his way down her body until his knees met the wet porcelain of the tub and his mouth met her cunt. Firmly pressed against the shower wall, Julia gripped his hair and pressed his face into her cunt, licking her lips and moaning as the water ran down her face and chin and fell onto his shoulders and back.

His tongue explored what he imagined was equally as astonishing as the outside of her. He plunged shallow and deep, his hands caressing her thighs and ass and when she began to pull his hair and dig her fingernails into his shoulders, he caressed her to a sweet arrival on his lips.

His knees were sore from the hardness of the tub. His lips ached from the fervor of which he loved her. And when she couldn't move, she spoke.

"He closed on the house yesterday. I'll be leaving in a few days. This weekend at the latest."

Gil exhaled the words he couldn't say. He lifted his head and stared at her through blurred eyes. Her body was again exposed and he pressed his skin to hers. He kissed her breasts goodbye and pressed his face against her belly and wept.

In his study on an especially cool Tuesday, Gil sat behind his desk and listened to John Coltrane. Linda entered without knocking and stood behind his chair, caressing his neck.

"What's wrong, Gil? What's been on your mind this week?"

He struggled for the words. He thought of Julia's lips, her chin, her neck. Then he touched Linda's hand. "Just a painting I saw at an auction."

"Oh?" she feigned interest. "Did you bid?" Her inquiry was half-hearted and it was just as well.

"I did… and lost."

"Well, there'll be another." She patted his back sympathetically.

"I'm not so sure, Linda, I'm not so sure."

His shoulders slumped and he turned the music off. He got up from the chair and flipped off the lamp, leaving Linda in the dark.

NAKED NEW YEAR
by Dante Davidson

On New Year's Eve, Nicole told me to meet her at our neighborhood park at half-past eleven.

"Is there a party?" I asked.

Her glossy dark hair flipped around her face as she shook her head. "Not a *party* party," she explained, a little half-smile touching her lips.

"Then what?"

"Just be there. By our bench. And be on time."

Although I thought the request was out of the ordinary, that didn't mean I found it any less erotic. Nicole has her own sorts of ideas for how to celebrate the holidays. Rather than gorging on turkey on Thanksgiving, we shared a night filled with giving thanks in all sorts of wanton ways that would have made the Pilgrims spontaneously combust. There were no red construction paper hearts on Valentine's day, but pretty twisting candles dripping white wax upon our naked bodies. The Fourth of July was celebrated with sexual fireworks so great it took days for us to get our strength back. So knowing Nicole, I had the feeling that her idea of a New Year's fiesta was going to be a whole different sort of party than one in which the ball dropped.

And I was right.

At the designated meeting time, there was Nicole, waiting for me on the wooden bench where we had shared our first kiss nearly a year before The park was deserted at this hour— there is a posted sign near the front parking lot stating "No use between sunset and sunrise"—and the atmosphere was dreamy. This was our place. For our own private use.

Nicole had on a long black cloak pulled tight around her slender waist, but she shifted her legs as I got closer, letting me see that she was bare beneath the sumptuous fabric. That made me harder than I'd been on the walk over. Harder than I thought I actually could be.

"What time is it?"

"Half-past," I told her, "just like you said."

"But *exactly* what time?"

I checked my watch again. "Eleven thirty-two and eighteen seconds. Why?"

"The countdown," she explained matter-of-factly.

"You want to go home and watch on TV?" I was baffled. Why have me meet her here if she didn't want to stay and play?

"A different countdown," she explained. "Our own special way to celebrate."

I slid a hand into the opening of her coat, and my fingers met the warm, soft flesh of her breast. God, did her skin feel delicious. I wanted to pounce right on her, wanted to tear open her cloak, spread her out right there in the chill night air and have my way with her, but Nicole's dark eyes flashed at me in the moonlight, and I didn't move.

"What way?" I asked finally, since that's what she seemed to want.

"We'll have our own countdown," she said, "a countdown to coming."

Ah. That made sense. That sounded like my sweet little sex fiend. "You're not talking only about a mutual orgasm, are you?" I asked.

She shook her head.

"You want us to really ring in the New Year."

Now, she nodded.

"That's going to take some precision."

"Then we'd better get started," she said, parting her coat completely and letting me see her naked body, agleam against the velvet background of her long winter cloak. I knew she must be cold, but she didn't tremble at all. Her cheeks were rosy from the night air, and also from the excitement of being outside, in a public place, about to do a very private thing.

Even though I knew we were all alone, I turned my head to make sure. Way across the grassy space, stood a row of houses. Some were festively lit, and I could hear the sound of muted music. Half a football field away in the other direction was a public pool, closed for the winter months. Everything else was quiet and empty.

"Ready?" Nicole whispered.

I nodded and dropped to my knees, leaning into her, drinking in her scent before bringing my mouth to the split of her legs. She twined her fingers in my hair and pulled me back. She wasn't going to let me start with dessert. That was clear from her take-charge attitude. Reluctantly, I moved upward, positioning myself between her legs as I started by kissing her collarbone, then her breasts, one then the other, spending time to warm her all over as I made her wait for the pleasure of my tongue. Or, really, she made *me* wait. I knew this wasn't difficult for her at all. I was ravenous, ready to dine, but Nicole was enjoying the suspense. She likes the thrill of the build-up. She's taught me a lot about waiting in our eleven months together. I should have known she'd want to make this evening last.

As Nicole began to make soft cooing noises, I continued my tantalizing trip down her body. When I brought my mouth forward again, I expected to feel her fingers in my hair, slowing me once more. But no. Now that I'd kissed my way along the treasure map, I was allowed to open the box and see the jewels within.

Nicole sighed and shivered as my tongue flicked out to touch her clit. I could feel how excited she was and that made me even more excited, myself. I was getting into this delayed gratification kick, and I teased her by moving away again, kissing her inner thighs, working down her lovely legs until she said, "No, please, baby. Don't be cruel..."

Back up I went, nipping at her pussy lips gently before ringing her clit with my lips. I expected to hear sighs of contentment, maybe a chorus of "Ohs" and "yes, baby, yesses." What I heard instead was, "Wait, Damon. What time is it?"

I held my watch up for her to see while I continued to flick my tongue against her clit, moving more rapidly now, trying to make her scream, or at least make her forget all about the coming New Year—or the New Year's coming. But I had no luck. Nicole can remain contained for the longest time. I like to make her melt, like to take her outside of herself.

"We have twenty minutes," she said, and I did catch a waver in her voice, so I knew my ministrations between her thighs were having some effect. "Here, come up on the bench with me."

She stood, spread her cloak along the bench, and then moved aside. I quickly lay down on top of the cloak-padded bench and took her back into my arms, but now, we were in a sixty-nine, with Nicole popping my fly and releasing my more-than-willing hard-on. Her ruby-slicked lips embraced the head of my cock, and I leaned back on the bench and swallowed hard. God, does my girl know how to give head. She's so good, that for several moments I forgot what I was supposed to be doing. But then I felt Nic's body wriggling on mine, and I realized how cold she must be, and I went back to warming her up with my mouth.

She was so juicy and wet, and I licked and lapped at her as she introduced my cock to a series of generous head-bobbing sucks from between her gorgeous lips. I was moaning now, and I knew Nicole liked the way my voice vibrated against her. I could tell from the way she moved her ass back and forth, and then pressed herself firmly down on my mouth. I found the silver rings adorning her pussy lips and licked and tugged at these until Nicole groaned. Then I thrust my tongue deep inside of her and fucked her like that, my hands on her ass, spreading her cheeks wide apart and strumming my fingertips against her asshole. In response, Nicole rubbed her head back and forth on me, so that I could feel her hair tickling my most sensitive skin as she continued to give me the blow job of the year. She tricked her tongue up and down my shaft, then drew the rounded head between her lips once more, sucking fiercely.

I would have loved to have relaxed right then and come deep down her throat, but now I was into the game, and I brought my wrist up and flicked the button so I could see the time: 11:49. We had eleven minutes left, and there was no way I was going to give in to her before midnight—or let her give in to me.

I pulled away from her and put my hands around her waist. "Off," I hissed.

"You want me to stop?" she sounded startled, and I didn't blame her.

"I want you to stand and bend over the bench. I want your naughty ass high up in the air, so arch your back for me."

She moved quickly into position. I stood, as well, kicked off my boots and stripped out of my shirt and jeans. Now, we were two naked beings, wild things in the middle of this deserted space. I anchored her with my hands on her hips and slid the head of my well-moistened cock between her thighs. Nicole sighed harshly and pushed back on me, and I sensed that she was testing me when she slid one hand between her thighs to cup and cradle my balls. That wasn't playing fair. We had nearly eight more minutes of prime-fucking time. If she teased my balls like that, I wasn't going to last. But I wasn't going to tell her to stop, either, because it felt amazing. So I played right back, grabbing hold of her long dark hair in one hand and pulling her head back. Nicole likes when I manhandle her, and I turned her head to the side and roughly kissed her, making her forget that she was trying to push me over the edge.

When she was breathless from the kiss, I released her and started to stroke her, in and out, but now I punctuated each thrust with a stinging spank on her upturned ass. Nicole loves a good spanking, especially when she's being fucked. She groaned at the feel of the punishing blows, and then rewarded me with pulsing contractions of her cunt. Each thrust won a spank. Each spank won a squeeze. We were both trying to outdo the other, until I forgot all about the little contest of wills and could think only about the outrageous pleasure.

And that's when Nicole hissed, "Damon—wait!"

I looked down at my watch, and said, "No, baby. It's okay. Come on. Ten, nine, eight..."

She shuddered all over. I could see she was trying her best to obey.

"...seven...six...five..."

We could hear the noise from the neighboring party increase in volume, and then we were coming together, riding together, fucking with as much force as I can ever imagine. It was as if I could see a halo of fire around us, our energies connected as we brought each other over the crest...and into the New Year.

"That was amazing," I sighed, aware that I could see my breath in the air. I reached down and quickly bundled Nicole up again in her coat. Then I slid my own jeans back on and took hold of her, bringing her onto my lap for a warm embrace.

"Yeah," she purred back at me, head resting on my shoulder. "But if you think *that* was fun, just wait until you see what I've got planned for Groundhog Day."

HER BIRTHDAY SUIT
by Kate Laurie

"Stop looking so scared, Mina. You know I would never do anything to hurt you." Marcy's impatient reassurance did nothing to calm my fears.

"Will you at least tell me why I'm tied to the bed?" I asked my best friend hopefully. I sighed when there was no response. I had met her and Grace at the posh hotel expecting nothing more than my typical birthday present. Every year they would rent a room at a luxurious hotel and we would stay up all night drinking good wine and critiquing porn films. This time, however, as soon as I had entered the room, the two girls had blindfolded me and ushered me onto the king-sized bed. Then they had proceeded to tie my wrists and ankles to the bedposts with what felt like satin.

"I wish I could stay and watch, but I promised Marcy I wouldn't," Grace whispered to me excitedly.

"Wait," I urged her quietly. I struggled to hide a grin when I heard her stop and then move closer. I tried to look terrified, "Please let me know what's happening," I begged pitifully.

"I can't."

"Won't you just tell me what the two of you are planning?" I held my breath as I waited for her to come to a decision.

"All right. But try to look surprised or Marcy will know that I didn't keep my mouth shut." I nodded in eager agreement. "In about five minutes a man will be arriving whose only instructions are to sexually please you in every imaginable way." She sighed. "I'm so jealous. I hope you guys are as creative when *my* birthday comes around."

Just then Marcy came back into the room, so Grace hurried away.

I lay on the bed in shock. I'm not a sexually inhibited person, and this was every girl's fantasy. But my lack of control frightened me. Bound to the bed and subject to the desires of a stranger made me tremble. "Can you please come over here, Grace?" I called in a voice that shook just a tiny bit.

"What is it, Mina?" Grace asked cheerfully.

"Closer," I whispered, lowering my voice until she had to sit on the bed beside me to hear it. "How do you know this guy isn't a psycho?"

"We would never leave you in the hands of a stranger!" Grace assured me in a shocked voice. "Don't worry. It's someone we trust to take care of you very carefully and thoroughly." After uttering those confusing words, she left again.

I frowned as I mentally replayed what she had said. Someone they knew and trusted. I almost would have preferred a stranger. I considered the male acquaintances we had. Not one seemed like the type of man they would have chosen to approach about something this bizarre and personal. A knock on the door scattered my thoughts and sent my heart racing.

"Come in and make yourself comfortable," Marcy's low voice called out happily. She let out a throaty laugh, "Is that your bag of goodies?"

I assume he must have nodded.

"I'm glad to see that you've come well prepared."

What did he bring? I struggled against my bonds one more time to no avail. I heard heavy footsteps coming towards me, and a large hand stroked my face. I froze and struggled to breathe normally.

"Don't squirm so, darling. These scarves are made of silk, but you'll still bruise your wrists if you struggle too much."

He continued to brush my hair back from my face as he said this. His voice was deep and textured like red wine, and it was also vaguely familiar. I tried to place it but came up blank. I jumped a little as he sat on the bed, and I felt the press of a jeans-clad leg against my side. I opened my mouth to speak, but he beat me to it.

"Goodbye, ladies. I should be gone by early tomorrow morning, but you may want to wait until noon or so before coming up. I have a feeling that Mina may be bit tired tomorrow." He ran his hand down my arm as he said that and I felt my skin prickle with goose bumps.

"Take good care of her tonight," Marcy instructed the mysterious man sternly. "Don't hold back at all, no matter how much she begs. I want this to be a one-night stand like no other for our Mina."

"Bye, honey, you can thank us tomorrow," Grace called out with a giggle as she shut the door behind them.

I wanted to cry out for them to come back, but I didn't. I knew that there wasn't a thing I could say that would change Marcy's mind. Instead, I turned to my captor with what I hoped was a winsome smile. "I won't say a word to them if you let me go. I'll make up an outrageously seductive story they'll believe, and I'll even pay you twice what they are," I offered hopefully. I felt his hands on my ankles and felt a surge of triumph. It faded when he simply tugged off my sandal. He moved to my other foot and did the same thing.

"A promise is a promise. I can't leave until you are absolutely satisfied." He punctuated the statement with a small kiss to my ankle that sent chills racing up my body and a traitorous clenching between my thighs. He laughed as if aware of my reaction, then casually asked, "Is that a favorite outfit you're wearing?"

It took me a moment to register what he had said since it seemed so irrelevant. "No, actually it's not. It's just comfortable." I found myself trying to justify it, and I rolled my eyes in disgust. There was no reason for me to defend my choice of clothing to this man.

"Good," he answered shortly and then I felt a touch of cold metal on my skin and the sound of fabric tearing.

"What the hell are you doing?" I asked furiously. He didn't answer and didn't stop. I felt him cut through the waist and down the front of the long skirt I had worn. Then he lifted my rear up and swept the fabric out from under me and began cutting off my tank top. "Stop right this minute. Aren't you supposed to be seeing to my pleasure?"

"How am I going to do that when you're fully clothed?" he asked with a sexy laugh.

I decided not to respond, tensing when I felt the scissors slide against my hip as he cut the sides of my panties. I felt a shiver of apprehension and hoped my friends were right to trust this man. A moment later, he snipped the straps of my bra and undid the clasp. He slipped the garment off my shoulders and I cursed the vulnerability of my position. I wanted to murder Marcy and Grace.

"I really wish you wouldn't struggle so. The last thing I want is for you to chafe your wrists."

I forced myself to stay still, and I listened to the sound of him undressing.

"I want you to know that I'm not going to do anything that you truly do not want tonight. This doesn't mean that you can just tell me to go home. Instead it means that if there are particular pleasures that you are uncomfortable with just tell me and I will stop. Now, why don't I get to know your body a little better." Indeed as soon as he finished his speech, he slid his nude body next to mine and rested his hand on my damp mound.

"Oh good, I expected that this would excite you," he laughed in delight.

"Are you going to let me take off my blindfold?" I asked him calmly. I was trying not to react to the long fingers that teased my plump lips. I was ashamed of my body's easy desire. Already I felt the tips of my breasts tightening and more moisture gathering below.

"No, Mina, that is something I can't allow. You know me, and I don't think you'd be able to experience the pleasure as freely if you knew who I was." He paused and ran his hand in a long caress from my shoulder to my hip. "It would be difficult for both of us after, as well, and I don't want to cause you any awkwardness."

I was becoming more confused by the minute. So he was someone I saw at least occasionally, and he didn't think I'd be able to enjoy myself as much if I knew who he was. I suddenly lost the ability to think reasonably as he leaned over and licked my right nipple with his tongue. I cried out despite myself.

"Yes, Mina that's the type of sound I want to hear from you tonight. No more questions and no more worries. Now, I'm going to give you a massage to relax you." He scooted down to the bottom of the bed and placed his hand on my ankle. "Can I trust you not to kick me?"

"I won't kick you," I promised quickly. I was feeling more aroused by the moment, and I no longer had any desire to escape.

He untied the scarf from around my ankle and placed my foot in his lap. I couldn't help but move my foot a little in a small upward stroke along his inner thigh. He laughed but said nothing. He leaned across me and I felt the rasp of his pubic hairs against the sole of my foot. Curious as to his endowment, I attempted to investigate with my foot, but this time he caught my foot with his hand.

"No more of that now, Mina. I'm about to rub oil into your feet and calves, and it would be hard for me to concentrate if you kept that up. So please be good, and perhaps I'll be able to untie you completely." He slipped one oiled hand up my calf and leaned forward to plant a chaste kiss on my upper thigh. "Promise me you'll be good, Mina."

I shivered in anticipation and desire, but I managed to squeak out a quiet reassurance, "I'll be good." I couldn't prevent a moan of delight as I felt his large warm hands begin working on my foot. He was using a liberal amount of the oil, and it felt divine. When he ran his blunt fingernails across my arch I felt my entire body jerk in a combination of pleasure and surprise. He removed his hands and I attempted to sit up, forgetting the restraints for a moment. "Please don't stop," I told him breathlessly. "I promise not to move at all."

"I'm just pouring more oil into my hands so I can start on your calf." He slid both his hands all the way up my leg stopping just before my wet and swollen lips. He gave a small laugh and his breath caused my clitoris to swell in impatient desire. "At least I can be reasonably assured that my services have been appreciated so far."

He poured a small puddle of oil onto my shin and I sighed at its delicious warmth. He lifted my foot into his lap again and began easing all the tight muscles in my calf. He had amazingly sexy hands. They were long fingered and strong with just a hint of calluses. The rough texture of his fingertips felt delicious against the silkiness of the oil and the sensitive smoothness of my skin. He poured some more oil onto my thigh and began rubbing it in the most leisurely way imaginable. He was driving me mad with lust. I had thought that his hands on my calves were heaven, but this was hell. Every sweep of his large hands brought him higher.

"I'm relaxed enough. I command you to bring me satisfaction now." I felt like a fool as I stated the request imperiously, but I attempted to maintain a look of haughty dignity beneath my blindfold. I gasped when he slid a slick hand up my thigh and gently teased the crease between my thighs.

"Sorry, I am here to pleasure you, that's true enough. I was instructed however to bring you to release only when it would be unbearably cruel to wait a moment longer, and I think a little more anticipation will do you good." He began massaging my thigh again, but then he paused, "But I could give you a little something to tide you over, since my desire probably matches your need."

Then he leaned forward and my world exploded.

His tongue was the most divine thing to ever touch me. He found my pulsing clit on the first try and I embarrassingly climaxed immediately. His tongue was incredibly flexible. I found myself wishing I could take back my orgasm in order to keep that exquisite torture continuing. He didn't stop, however, and as he expertly alternated between kissing my lips and my clit he brought me to the cusp once again. I thrashed as much as was possible within my binds, and cried out intelligible encouragements. Then he stopped. I gasped for air and waited desperately for his damp mouth to return, but was disappointed.

"You taste wonderful," he told me, slightly breathless. "I hope you're ready for a long night," he warned me with mock sternness. "I had promised myself to resist bringing you to climax for at least three hours, and it's only been one hour."

He pinched my clit between his fingers and I bucked my hips in an unpreventable response. "I couldn't resist you, though. All spread out on the bed, with your pink lips all swollen and dripping wet beneath your damp curls. I tried to ignore you, but I've wanted you too long." He snapped his mouth shut after this, and I realized that he'd given away more than he meant to.

"Are you completely sure you won't let me take the blindfold off?" I begged him piteously. I was amazingly curious now. I felt that I must know who he was. There was something absolutely exhilarating about knowing that a man had secretly lusted after my body and had been given the chance to act out all of his fantasies. I couldn't imagine anyone I knew being capable of the expert foreplay this man was exhibiting. I once again searched my brain for possibilities but this man seemed much too sensual and experienced to be anyone of my acquaintance.

"Sorry, darling I can't do that." He dropped his voice down until I could feel it like liquid silk all over my body. "Don't you think it adds to the experience? A little helplessness and intrigue thrown in for spice? I have you completely at my mercy and you must rely on the judgment of your two friends and none of your own. I find your unconquerable passion quite exhilarating myself," he confessed into my ear. A chill ran down my body and I felt my nipples tighten to a point of near pain. "So how old are you now, Mina?"

I forced myself to focus enough to answer.

"I will be twenty-six at ten till midnight." I gasped when I felt his hands smooth the warmed oil all over my sensitive breasts. "Oh, god."

He laughed and rolled both of my aching nipples at once. "No more talking, Mina. The only sounds I will accept for the next few hours are those of passion. Now relax and enjoy your birthday present." I was about to explain that I would talk if I wanted to but just then he pressed my breasts together and took both of my nipples into his mouth at once. I decided he was right. This was a once in a lifetime opportunity and I was going to take advantage of it.

For the first time I was actually glad for his blindfold. While he leaned over me and teased my nipples mercilessly, I scooted down as far on the bed as my restraints would allow.

Then I began to rub desperately on his thigh. After a moment, I felt him take his mouth off my nipples in surprise.

"Move a little closer. I need more friction," I gasped out. He silently acquiesced, even shifting over a little until I had perfect access. I groaned in approval and achieved a delicious rhythm against his muscular leg.

I was strung so tight I thought I'd explode. All of my skin seemed on fire tonight. Being deprived of my sight made all of my other senses work overtime; and it was driving me wild. I relished the taste of the sweat on my upper lip. The salty tang of my skin mixed with our mutual desire to produce an exotic musk that I breathed in gratefully. The greatest increase was my sense of touch. It felt as though I had a million sensory nerves in every inch of my skin. The sensitivity that I normally only felt on my breasts, thighs, and neck had spread until my entire body quivered with every touch.

He leaned over and licked my lower stomach and I bucked my hips in ecstasy. His long tongue traced delicate designs onto my skin that caused my toes to curl with delight.

He began kissing a slow line of heat down my stomach until he stopped just above my thatch of brown curls. I thrust upward in desperation.

"Guess what, Mina? It's almost midnight. Happy birthday," he whispered the last right against my sex and the slight vibration of his mouth caused my hips to buck and my head to fall back in frustration.

"Please fuck me," I begged him. "Please!"

I wanted nothing more than to be filled to bursting by a large and thick cock. I just hoped he'd measure up to my needs.

"I'll do even better," he promised me mysteriously. He gave me one long slow lick that made me shiver. I frowned when I felt his weight leave the bed.

I heard him rummaging around in what I guessed was the bag that Marcy had referred to earlier tonight. Tonight? It was hard to believe that I had only been tied up for a few hours. It felt as though this had been my entire existence. This mix of pleasure and anxiety was intoxicating. I bit my lip as I wondered what he would do next.

"Lift your hips a little," he told me as I felt him sit next to me again. I obeyed, and he slipped a firm pillow beneath my lower back. I was now displayed quite obscenely for him, and I jumped a bit when I felt him spreading lubricant over my anus. "Shh, if you don't like it I'll take it out."

"Take what out?" I gasped as my question was answered. He slowly slipped a small dildo into me. I experimented by rocking my hips forward and was surprised when I felt it flex inside of me.

"What is that?" I gasped out.

"It's filled with oil so that it will contract and flex in time to your thrusts. Do you like it?" he asked me curiously.

I nodded in response and I could almost see his grin when he responded.

"Great, we are ready to begin then."

I was about to ask what we were going to begin, but I didn't get a chance. He untied my other foot, kissed my ankle where the scarf had been tied and then hoisted both of my legs onto his shoulders. His skin was incredibly hot, and as he slid up towards me, I smiled to find that he was covered in a fine sheen of sweat. He thrust his middle finger into me, and I jerked up sharply causing the dildo to rock pleasurably inside me. He began to tease my clitoris with his tongue, and I threw my head back in amazement. This was the most exquisite feeling imaginable. I felt as though I might actually explode. I wasn't surprised when I climaxed almost immediately. He didn't even pause however. He was working in a taxing rhythm that didn't give me a moment of relief. The dildo was a steady pressure from behind and his finger was just long enough to press into me at almost the same exact spot. The feeling of being filled from both directions would have been enough to bring me to another shattering climax all on it's own, but when he added his skilled tongue into the mix again it was nearly too much. It wasn't until my third climax had left me shivering and drenched in sweat that he stopped.

I was languorous and completely sated. I looked at him and gave a slow sleepy smile. I blinked as I recognized Marcy's cousin, Jude. I felt my mouth drop open as I realized that my blindfold must have slipped off during one of my shuddering orgasms. He had his eyes closed as he rested his head on my upper thigh. I admired his sexy mouth and tousled black hair for a moment before I spoke up.

"Why, Jude, you could have done this for my birthday long ago."

Jude sat straight up in surprise. He met my eyes and winced. "Are you mad at me, Mina?" he asked hesitantly.

I looked at him in silent appraisal. His upper body was gleaming with sweat and his mouth was wet from my own juices. I licked my lips and sighed. "Not at all. Now are you ready to come up here and fuck me for real?" I purred.

He looked up at me in amazement and then grinned. "With pleasure." He reached above me and untied both of my wrists. He entered me with one swift thrust that brought me to the edge once again. I smoothed my hands down his muscular back and then gripped his hips.

He pounded into me with abandon, causing the dildo to tease me relentlessly. I was truly amazed when I came yet again, and I felt more than a little grateful to my friends for setting this up. I flung my arms out to the sides and peered up at Jude with a look of contemplation. "I hope you know that I'll be expecting this on more days then my birthday," I warned him.

"I think that can be worked out," he promised me gravely. "In fact," he told me as he entered me again, "I think I'll start right now."

SKIN ON SKIN
by Saskia Walker

Jade attempted to quell her erratic breathing. She began to walk down the narrow passageway, eyeing the purple-painted walls that were lit by triangles of hazy light. The beat of a bass guitar sounded through the walls and the floor. The atmosphere grew heavier as she reached the door at the end of the passage, resonant with a heady mix of heat, sound and scent. Her heart rate quickened. She paused, noticing that the paint was cracked in the top left-hand corner of the heavy black door, lifting and peeling away, revealing the bare wood beneath. Jade had a keen eye for such things. That was why she had come to The Cave that night, to relish the surface coverings, and that which lay beneath.

She glanced down at her outfit, hoping it would blend in with what she would find beyond the door. A cut-off latex top, sleeveless and skin-tight, left her midriff bare. A leather miniskirt was cinched around her hips, zippered from waist to hem at front and back. Shiny soft plastic boots clung to her legs, like skins on her skin. The decadent outfit gave her cover; it also gave her nerve. She lifted her chin. Jade was a shy but deep-down determined sort. She had an insatiable curiosity for all things sexual, and she could insinuate herself most places with utter stealth.

The door opened and a figure darted past her. Jade took a deep breath at the scene beyond. The room was full of bodies, moving, dancing, whispering against one another. The sound was vibrant, industrial dance music that sliced through the senses. It invaded her body with its powerful, undulating rhythms. A pulse point rapidly began to pound inside of her. Flashes of brilliant color broke the pools of darkness that met her eyes: a transparent neon shirt flickering with movement, a streak of deep scarlet satin hanging low on a tattooed back, white skin shining beneath black straps buckled across a dancer's back.

Strobe lights sprang to life, flashing a series of frozen images of the crowd in negative versions of themselves, before submerging them again into a heaving dark mass of dancing. Fetish. Alternative. Jade smiled. How could she not love a fashion that revealed the body with such erotic candor? A wave of heat was building between her thighs.

She slipped easily amongst the bodies, unseen, brushing against them, her eyes taking in each and every clinging fabric, wistfully peeling them away in her mind. There was nothing like luxurious, fetishistic fabrics to reveal the erotic potential of the body beneath. After seeing a TV feature on the London fetish and alternative scene, Jade had abandoned the mainstream clubs she'd gone to with her girlfriends and the gang from the office. She was now working her way through a list of London alt.clubs with a mixture of arousal and trepidation. Had she known how tempting an eager innocent was to the fetish generation, her arousal might have reached boiling point before she'd even set foot inside.

A woman in PVC sidled past her. Jade closed her eyes and breathed appreciatively. Like latex, PVC molded to the skin by virtue of the heat it met. The material outlined the body, emphasizing every naked inch of skin beneath, every curve, every ridge. Peeling warm PVC or latex off after a night constricted in the body-hugging material was one of Jade's most pleasurable indulgences. The way the malleable, synthetic material lifted away from the skin beneath was exquisite. Shocked naked, the cold air raced over the surface of the body, every nerve ending wired with sensation. It was one of the most delicious stimulations she could imagine, and she wrestled with fantasies about sharing it with another, allowing someone else to peel back her synthetic skins and reveal what lay beneath. She had tread this path alone; a tourist silently observing, her imagination running wild.

Jade headed towards the bar, a strip of smooth black onyx dividing the space between two dance floors. She leaned over it and gave her order to the barmaid, a woman with a crown of bleached hair and heavily kohl-lined eyes. The woman was dressed in a white sheath of a top, lycra. It revealed her nipples, rock hard and aggressive on her lean chest. Jade turned away and drank her wine quickly. Her fingers traced the cool line of the bar and her eyes flickered over the scene in front of her. There was an attitude of open appreciation about the place, everyone was eyeing each other and preening for the view of others. Jade put the empty glass on the bar and began to edge round the crowd. When she came upon the ladies' toilets, she entered and closed on the mirror to check her make-up.

The bright light made her look paler than ever, and she reached into her bag for her lipstick. Despite her dark hair, her skin and lashes were very pale. Another lick of red strengthened her mouth and she unwound a tiny lid liner and began to outline her eyes. Her hands trembled slightly and the line escaped her control.

"Damn," she breathed, and dropped the liner on the shelf in exasperation.

"Let me do it for you," a voice behind her suggested. She turned and saw a woman with a shock of black hair standing some five feet away from her. She was watching Jade with a smile on her lips. Jade glanced at the scarlet dress that clung to her statuesque figure and remembered the flash of scarlet on the dance floor. It was heavy satin and pooled in all the right places, between her breasts, into the groin, around the thighs. Jade flushed when she realized the woman was smiling at her, as if aware of her wandering eyes. Was she being very obvious about looking? She glanced away. The woman sidled forward and picked up the lid liner.

"When I was a teenager, I used to do make up for all my girlfriends. Now, lower your eyelids." Jade complied, and her downcast eyes took in the red toenails that peeped from the toe of the woman's low-slung black suede shoes. The black straps that bound her ankles emphasized the lines of her ankles.

"They used to come to me, because I could do this really easily on others, although I could never get it right on myself." Jade felt the smooth damp line cross her right eye in a quick swoop. "Of course, the intervening years have improved my aim somewhat." The second line was drawn. "There you go."

"Thanks," Jade murmured. She looked admiringly at the woman. Her hair was thick and cropped into spiky layers around her face. Her eyes were almost black and heavily fringed, her full sensual mouth painted in a deep plum color.

"I'm Nadia," she said. Then, with a knowing smile she added, "You haven't been to The Cave before, have you?"

"Jade," she said, before adding meekly, "no, I haven't."

"I thought not; I'd remember you."

Jade felt her cheeks heat. There was something very direct and playful about the woman. Nadia reached over to Jade's upswept hair and pulled out a few strands to hang free, framing her face. The back of Nadia's finger stroked against Jade's cheek. Jade shivered with delight, and Nadia smiled.

"Why don't you come along with me, Jade? I know what lovelies you should talk to and whom you should ignore." Nadia linked Jade's arm and before Jade knew what had happened she found herself clinched against the lush, inviting woman who led her across the club with real purpose. The arm that linked her was warm and silky-smooth. The satin dress moved as if it would slide off at any moment. Jade swallowed hard.

Nadia led her over to the bar and towards two men.

"Look what I just picked up in the ladies," Nadia said. Their heads turned in unison towards Jade. Jade noted the inference in Nadia's comment. Had she been picked up? Well, she supposed she had. She felt herself blush, again, and looked at Nadia to avoid the curious stares of the men.

"This is Jade. Jade, meet my fellow creatures of the night. The bleach baby is Carl, the other is Sam." Jade forced herself to follow Nadia's arm as it languidly gestured towards the two attractive men. Carl had long hair, bleached almost white. He wore tight black jeans and a flowing shirt, tantalizingly unbuttoned, revealing the lean muscle of his chest and abdomen. He was incredibly handsome, with a sexual ambiguity that was fascinating. He smiled warmly, as if her joining them was the most natural thing in the world.

Sam was darker in coloring, with short black hair. Confidence emanated from him, in the way he held himself and the way he looked at Jade: his eyes raked over her with blatant speculation. He was more overtly masculine than Carl and his body was draped over the bar in a way that seemed to invite a sexual response from Jade. She smiled, nervously. His chest looked broad and strong beneath the black t-shirt he had on. Her heart missed a beat; he was wearing PVC trousers. She tried to drag her eyes away from the rather impressive ridge outlined beneath the fly.

"What a find," he murmured. His eyes continued to rove over Jade's body, taking in the line of her breasts beneath the tight latex top and the inviting zip up the middle of her short leather skirt.

Nadia noticed the exchange, chuckled and said: "Come on, let's dance."

Jade took a deep breath and willed herself to follow. This was it; this was what she had secretly both feared and desired: she'd been picked up by a bunch of people who looked like their clothes were about to fall off at any moment!

They pressed into the crowd to find a space. The movements of the other dancers transmuted into Jade's body, starting her own responses to the music. The foursome found a small space and made it larger with their bodies. Nadia danced like a stealthy cat, often closing her eyes to trace the music more precisely with her body, following where it led. Jade could feel the beat spread up through the floor and pound right inside her, in that inner flesh that was so sensitive to stimulation of a sensual nature.

When a synthesized thread sprung up, Jade felt Nadia's hands brush against her body like gossamer strands, arousing the naked skin at her waistline. Nadia laughed suddenly, her wide mouth full and delighted, then Jade felt arms slide around her from behind and Sam's face appeared over her shoulder. His body was pressed against her back, taut and wired. He moved his body with hers, swaying to the music. He slid his hands over her hipbones as he nuzzled against her neck. Her head fell back when she felt his mouth against the sensitive skin of her throat. Nadia moved forward, her arms trailing out to them. Jade shut her eyes; she wanted the sensations to last forever.

"Time to go," Nadia said, and the men responded immediately.

They scooped her up and piled into a taxi bound for Nadia's apartment. Somewhere at the back of her mind Jade wondered why she was going with them. She pushed her momentary doubts away; the adventure was just too tempting to be denied.

Nadia's home was the entire top floor of an old Victorian house, converted into a huge studio. It was a gaunt space with a couple of doorways leading off on one side. Filling one side of the huge floor space were a pile of cushions and rugs focused around a low copper table that held a dish, candles and a lamp. Nadia went over to the table and lit some floating candles in the dish. She flung herself back on the cushions on the far side of the table, waving Carl closer.

Sam arranged himself on the cushioned floor, and Jade sat down near him. She watched the wavering candlelight cast shadows across his collarbone and creeping patterns around his throat. It was like an invitation to touch him. He turned his head suddenly, and caught her gaze with a smile. She smiled, nervously, and glanced away.

What on earth was she doing here, she asked herself, but she soon forgot the question when she saw Nadia grab Carl around the neck, pulling his mouth to hers. Jade watched as their black and red clothes and their black and blonde hair entwined across the cushions. She felt Sam's hand slide around her waist and looked around as he caught her mouth with his, a slow lingering kiss arresting her movement. His mouth brushed over hers, then he kissed her deep. She trembled. He inclined her body back on the cushions and crept closer, his tongue teasing into her mouth as it opened to him.

Jade heard the movements of the other two and laughter. Unable to help herself, she drew her mouth from Sam's and turned to look as the black and red clothes entwined again. Nadia had pinned Carl to the floor, straddling his hips and holding his shoulders down. He struggled up against her body, bucking his hips and lifting her. Nadia was slowly pulling the shirt off him, chuckling all the time. Dear god, she was undressing him in front of them all! Each slow, revealing tug on the shirt aroused Jade more. Confusion nettled her. She flushed with embarrassment, instinctively closing her eyes and turning her face away.

"Don't you want to see?"

Her eyes snapped open.

Sam was smiling down at her, his expression provocative. *Yes*, she thought. *Yes, she did want to see*. She wanted to see them naked, she wanted them to see her, too. She forced herself to turn back.

Carl was flat on his back, his arms out at to the sides. Nadia had pulled the shirt off him, revealing his lean chest and the sinuous twists of muscles in his arms. Jade was riveted. Nadia lowered her head to his chest and teased his nipples with her tongue. He arched up. Her hands roamed over his body in deliberate, knowing movements.

"What is it that you want?" Nadia asked in a low voice as she leaned over him. Carl bowed his body up to her, his head falling back, his eyes tightly shut. "No! You must tell us all!" Nadia said, and gave a thoroughly wicked laugh.

"You," Carl said quietly, his eyes still closed. "I want you, Nadia." She fell forward to kiss his mouth.

Jade wondered if she should feel as if she was intruding, but didn't. She felt part of the undressing, part of the arousal.

"Jade," Nadia called in a low voice as she lifted her mouth from Carl's. She turned and looked at Jade with a suggestive smile. "I want you to hold him down for me." Nadia leaned forward and pinned his arms by the wrists above his head. She jerked her head, indicating Jade take over.

Jade was spellbound. She rolled away from Sam and crept over on her hands and knees. She took Carl's wrists into her control. His torso was a streak of white against the dark floor, pinned at wrist and hip by the two women. Nadia bent over his naked chest, licking his skin, her hands roaming around his body. He moaned, and his arms twisted in Jade's grip. Nadia moved down his body, undoing his jeans, hauling them down his legs, laying him bare. His cock bounced up, hard and eager. Nadia's head lowered. He writhed suddenly and Jade held his wrists tighter. His body arched, and then began to stir in response to Nadia's mouth on his cock.

Jade gasped when she felt a sudden movement at her back. Sam was standing behind her. She glanced around at him. He smiled at her and knelt down, squatting with his knees around the outside of hers, enclosing her body with his, his hands caressing her latex-covered breasts as she leaned over the prone man on the floor. She relaxed into the caress, her hips swaying back to nestle against his.

Nadia was pleasuring Carl with long slow plunges. Jade had never seen another woman giving head before, and she watched, mesmerized. Carl's arms lifted and struggled beneath Jade's hands, his head moving gently from side to side as his body went with the rhythm of Nadia's mouth. Nadia suddenly climbed over him, one knee on either side of his hips, hovering above his erect cock. Jade held her breath and watched as Nadia stretched up and lifted the heavy red satin, slowly pulling it up over her head. The fabric moved with a heavy swish over her body, lifting like a theater curtain to reveal the delights beneath.

Nadia threw the dress on the floor and looked down at the man she was conquering,. She was entirely naked, her body only adorned by the tattoos that crept around her shoulder from her back. Her naked body looked glorious in the candlelight, opulent and pale, but powerful, like a demon sex goddess. Her eyes were bright with lust, her lips parted with anticipation. She took Carl's cock in one hand and began to lower herself onto it. As the juncture of the naked bodies closed together, Jade swore it was a sight she would savor forever.

She felt Sam's hands moving and then his fingers began to peel her latex top up. She groaned her pleasure, her arms lifting to assist. Needles of sensation raced across the warm skin when it was exposed to the air. Her body shivered with delight. He rested his head into the back of her neck, growling at her reaction. She settled back into his lap; she could feel the bulk of his cock between her buttocks, pushing up against her sex. She wanted to feel it, wanted to feel his skin on hers.

When the latex top was gone, he rested his hands around her breasts, molding them. The sensations between his skin and hers was electric. Nadia smiled at them, her eyes running over Jade's body appreciatively. The fact that they were all looking at her was like fuel to her fire. Her head went back, her mouth opening, her hips began to move on Sam's. Jade was desperate to be part of this. She was watching Nadia fucking Carl; she was moving her hips in time with Nadia's

"Take your shirt off," she whispered to Sam.

"Gladly."

She cried out when she felt the skin of his chest against her back.

"For fuck's sake, woman, that zipper's driving me wild."

Jade chuckled, the tension mercifully breaking for a moment, and leaned forward so that he could unzip her skirt, splitting it open to reveal her buttocks, bare but for the strip of G-string she wore. She heard his murmur of pleasure as he unzipped himself, freeing his cock. Her heart began to race again. With one finger, he pushed the G-string aside and touched her slit, drawing a line of delicious torture from front to back. He weighed her clit between two fingers, massaging it quickly from beneath. She was bent forward, right over Carl's face, her breasts hanging down towards him. He watched the show with glazed eyes, one woman fucking him frantically, another naked and whimpering with pleasure above him.

Sam began to edge his cock inside Jade. He was hard and felt very big. He nudged his way in to her, easing her open to take his girth. She whimpered as he filled her, then physical need took over and she pressed right down onto its glorious bulk. The contrast between his warm skin and the cool sticky PVC covering his thighs was too divine. His hands guided her hips, and she began to ride him with abandonment, the feeling of his chest against her back and the sticky pull of the PVC on her bare legs adding their own frissons of pleasure throughout her body.

Nadia was moving frantically on Carl, her fingers clawing at him. Jade could see that they were both about to come. She fell forward again, onto his mouth, plunging her tongue into it and kissing him deep. She gasped when the movement forced Sam's cock up against the front wall of her sex, hitting the spot with uncanny accuracy. The tension in her sex was building. He began to rut her hard from behind. With each stroke, she plunged her tongue deeper against Carl's. He bucked and came and as he did so his mouth reached up to Jade, meeting her kiss and holding her. Sam pulled at her hips, his cock wedging in tight; she cried out against Carl's mouth when she began to spasm inside, her sex clenching. Sam hauled her body back up against him, his cock deep and hard against her while she came. Her whole body shuddered and he swore low and long, his cock pumping inside her.

She wilted gratefully into the embrace of his arms. Nadia had climbed across Carl's chest with a line of sticky kisses. Jade watched as they kissed, her body still rocking against Sam's. She glanced back. His mouth was too inviting, she turned her body and leaned into it again. His hands moved lightly over her body, making her reach for his touch.

"Do you want to come home with me?" he asked, "I live downstairs." He kissed her again, deeply. He was extremely attractive and his kisses held the promise of more, unhurried passion. She looked down at his half-undressed body. It demanded further attention. She took another deep breath and then smiled at him.

Jade was more than ready to help him shed the rest of his night skins.

BARE TO THE WAIST
by Alex M. Quinlan

I have a small office, more a closet than anything else. You don't need much else when you work alone on the night shift. There are nights when my work goes so smoothly that there's really nothing for me to do. When that happens, my mind is on my lovers and my computer journal is open, collecting the thoughts they have engendered. There's one in particular... I can almost see him when I close my eyes, the candle-glow making gold of his hair, sparking the gold highlights in his eyes....

He greeted me at the door with a robe on, smiling just short of a smirk, and once the door closed he dropped the robe to the floor. It was obviously a practiced motion, and it revealed nothing more than a silky collar and bow tie. Somehow, it just emphasized his nakedness, his tan skin and the minimal white around his intensely grab-able tight ass. Despite the fledgling Dom efforts at 'cool' and 'control' that he'd been trying to foster in me, I stood there lost in the sight of him, grinning like a completely witless fool.

I have no memory of how we got to his room, or if I risked embarrassing him in passing in front of a window. He waved me into his room and closed the door behind us, proper courtesy; by the time he turned around, I had sat on the end of the bed and was looking around to give myself time to acquire some couth. The myriad of candles, sitting on every flat surface, lent a glow to the entire room: stars of light to set the mood. They gleamed off every polished surface, highlighting his hair and tan, glinting off the polished wood of his furniture.

He stepped closer, looking at me solemnly, and, after a deep breath and a searching gaze, knelt at my feet and reached up to unbutton my blouse. Obedient to a gesture, he left it tucked in and falling open in graceful curves to outline my tattletale tits, my nipples up hard and bright, all but holes in my satin bra.

I lay back, half reclining on my elbows at the end of the bed, and watched him with my newly-practiced predator's gaze. He untied my shoes and gently pulled them off, setting them out of the way. My slippery nylon socks followed. After another glance for permission, he hesitantly took the edges of my wrap skirt and draped them out of the way; I could see his eyes widen when he found a notable lack of underwear. His nostrils flared as the scent of my arousal hit him, and, with a last look at my uncontrollably grinning face, he sat back, away from me, and took my foot in his hands and started to kiss my ankle, lightly, slowly, teasingly.

I watched him, still not quite able to believe this was all happening, that he was waiting for my permission before acting, that I had given him permission for this 'service,' which was only what we'd done a delicious number of times before. We'd gone from "What an interesting idea..." to him at my feet in a matter of weeks. The feeling was still very much "What the hell are we doing?" but the trembling arousal running through me was the hottest thing I'd felt in years.

His breath and lips and tongue were so light that the only thing that kept the sensation from tickling was the intense eroticism of the entire scene. He used his hands to massage the outside of my leg as he worked his way up the inside with his mouth. It was a delicious contradiction, his lips making my muscles jump and quiver, and his hands trying to relax and smooth them. Almost in sections, he ran his dark golden beard lightly over my skin, then kissed me lightly with just his lips, and then touched his tongue to my skin, lingering a moment before flitting onward. Over all, the sense of homage, of worship, charged the sensuality with power.

In a fit of sensory overload, I moaned and tried to pull my leg away, the trembling nearly overwhelming. But he merely set my leg down even as I did so and moved to the other one. This only made the overloading worse, as every touch there echoed as a lack on my other leg. Just watching was sweet torture for me; I could see him getting slowly closer to where I wanted him to be, to where all the sensation was flowing in a steady stream.

He reached my knee and moved around so that he was kissing and licking the soft, sensitive underside. Suddenly all was too much, and I threw my head back and closed my eyes, unable to bear the distraction. My leg quivered, all my muscles from the hips down taking part in this not-quite orgasm. With a last flick of his tongue, he massaged the top muscles of my thigh a bit longer, and then turned his attention back to my other leg.

He started a little higher on the calf this time, a little closer. A nuzzle, kiss, lick; a stroke of the tongue before moving on. Again. I fell flat on to the bed, unable to hold myself up anymore, and my hands went to my breasts, playing lightly with the nipples through my bra, trying to find his rhythm and match it. But he was too good a lover, too wise to give me anything to work with. Again he reached my knee, and *teased* the underside, this time stroking with his fingers also. Again my leg came, all the muscles reacting but my cunt still unsatisfied, getting more and more sensation-starved as the motions usually lavished on it were used elsewhere, to such wonderful effect.

His tongue stopped moving with quite such eloquence,

and his hands reached up to massage, to relax my leg. Only then did he continue, not switching, continuing up my thigh. He started using his nails, scratching lightly along the outside of my thigh, nuzzling, kissing, licking on the inside. He was far enough forward that I could begin to feel his hair on my cunt, a deliciously shivering sensation, when he again switched legs on me.

I moaned wildly and desperately tried to grab for his head, but he was already too far away. He started teasing again, this time just below the knee, and I couldn't control my lower body as all the muscles started twitching again. But he didn't linger long there this time, spending more time on the massage aspect than on the tease, and soon enough he was again on my thigh, scratching along the outside. Nuzzle, kiss, lick, stroke. My hands were glued to my tits, nipples up and hard, tingling and reinforcing what he was doing.

He moved his hands to either side of me, alternating legs with his tongue to slow the approach. I was so sensitized that his hair touching my nether lips created sensations usually associated with his fingers and tongue. I tried to move my legs apart to give him better access, but I couldn't seem to control them; it was as if he had charmed my legs like snakes, his light touch held me in place. He stroked along the outside of my leg, so light it was almost no touch at all, kissing on the inside, nuzzling my fur with his nose, but not putting anything near my clit, my lips, near any part of me that craved him.

I moaned softly as he reached under the skirt to grab my ass, kneading it with his hands as he nuzzled and licked up over my tummy to where the cloth blocked his progress. I couldn't stop moving my hips, rocking them slowly, trying to get some sensation into my cunt but caught in his slow non-rhythm. When he realized that he couldn't hold my hips still, he ran his fingers as close as he could to my slit, brushing the fur just barely enough to give sensation. He stroked down my thigh toward my knee a short way, and then started again near my slit. His feather kisses along my fur, in the crease of my hips, and on my thigh drove me crazy, and I kept moving my hips to try and catch his mouth. My hands on my tits stopped moving, my fingers just grabbing and stroking, pinching my nipples, pulling them hard, large and swollen in my need.

Finally, oh-so-forever finally, he ran his fingers across my cunt lips, feather light. A loud moan escaped me, a shiver that took over my entire body. He did it again, slipping between them slightly, and again and again, deeper each time. I tried to keep the volume down but my voice is always the first thing that escapes my control. I pulled my legs up onto the bed and, with that leverage, I moved my hips to try and make him touch me more—more intensely, more actively, more anything but this tease!

On the next stroke he found my clit, my sudden cry confirming his slowly surer touch. He took some of the fluid so freely available onto his finger and started, ever so lightly, to stroke across it, his other hand continuing the stroking of the surrounding lips, still just as lightly. He slipped one finger slightly inside, and I heard him chuckle softly as my muscles automatically attempted to grab it. He pulled his finger out again to a soft moan, and another, even louder, escaped my mouth as he bent to lick my lips.

"Yes, yes, please!" I whispered as he got closer to my clit and further in. But he prolonged this just as much if not more than everything else, following my squirming easily, foiling all my attempts to get him closer or harder or more intense.

Finally, he decided that I'd had enough of that tease. My body shaking and trembling, he took my clit between his lips, letting his tongue glide softly over the top, circling it and rubbing his lips across it. It was too much, or maybe just enough—he knew me well enough to tell by my cries, the gasping for breath and the extreme tension in my legs, that I was about to come. He grabbed my hips and hung on as my hands came down and grabbed his head, grinding myself against him so he couldn't pull away from me. He licked faster, and faster still, and suddenly the tension broke, my cries changed, deeper and more full-throated as the peak crested over me. My legs jerked and thrust my hips into the air, into his face, almost lifting him off his knees.

He didn't let go; he knew better. Neither his hands nor lips stopped although he shifted from short tonguing strokes to longer ones. As my bucking eased, he slipped one hand around and started to play with my slit, teasing me again with his fingertip just barely in my cunt. He didn't have to move his hand much, or his head for that matter, my hips were doing most of the work. He slipped his finger in deeper and felt around, and as he found the back of the pubic bone my orgasm restarted. And so he pulled it out a little, and stroked it in again. All the while, his tongue continued to lick my clit, with occasional forays to other places just for variety.

He teased me a while in this manner, slow stroke fingerfuck, and then added another finger and repeated the entire sequence. This time he started to fuck me with them, a definite rhythm; I couldn't keep from bucking my hips against his thrusts, and very quickly I came again, crying out as my body shook. This time the cries were more like whimpers. Before the orgasm faded he shifted his thumb up to my clit and as I started to come yet again I felt his head lift up, and I knew he was watching me.

With one hand flung over my head, the other was madly kneading and pinching my nipples. The cups of my bra were pushed out of place and my breasts looked very flushed. My entire body was rocking with the motion of my hips and my blouse had come untucked. He stood up, carefully keeping his hand moving, keeping me coming, and lay down on the bed next to me, on the side where my arm was over my head. When my hand moved to the other nipple, he started licking and sucking on my breast: flicking his tongue across the nipple, drawing his head back to lick a spiral away from it and back in, taking as much of it as possible into his mouth and sucking it as if he were a baby trying to suckle.

My insides clamped down on his hand and I completely exploded. All he could do was ride me, throwing a leg over one of mine and holding me on the bed. He lightened up on what he was doing with his thumb, and slowly, so slowly it all started to fade again. I grabbed his head and held it to my chest, but left him enough slack to move it around, playing with my tit. He ran his tongue down the side, trying to find the edge of the sensitive place under my arm. Without even really feeling it, I shrieked and bucked suddenly, that sudden overload letting him know he'd found it. He backed off, and again my moans changed to whimpers. My entire body quivered with every motion, every twitch of his fingers and flick of his tongue. He stroked my face, soft fingertips down my jaw-line and behind my ear. This new touch gained my attention, and I opened my eyes to look at him. The candles behind him made his disarranged hair glow, but his eyes were in shadow, hard to read, mysterious. I pulled him down to kiss, and the taste of myself on his lips sent me spinning again, orgasm coming and driving me again hard against his hand.

My orgasms were subsiding and I could feel my body slowing, my breathing heavier, simple physical tiredness gaining on me. He rubbed his lips against mine, and murmured, "Now? Please?" When I nodded weakly he kissed me once more, licking my lips, and levered himself up and over me.

Kneeling between my legs, the candles gilded his hair again, outlining him like some obedient godling, guiding his cock to me. He withdrew his fingers enough to hold open the lips and eased the head in, just past the ridge. This larger fullness seemed to renew my own need; immediately I started to moan, moving my hips towards him, trying to take more. Slowly, obediently but tortuously slowly for him, he let himself be engulfed.

He leaned over, hands next to my breasts, fully inside me, to lick and nuzzle my nipples, my throat, my neck and ears. My cunt gripped him just about his entire length, strongest near the base. Just when it seemed like I was going to come just from him being in me he started to move, slowly pulling out until he was just barely inside.

My whimpers changed, from incoherency to "No, please no, please!" as he pulled out. He seemed to hang there for a moment, and then thrust deep all at once. The world burst as I threw my head back with a scream, my legs lifting us both up and dropping us to the bed again in a sudden loss of muscle tone.

He let this happen, holding himself deep, and then flicked my underarms with his thumbs, once twice, again. My legs straightened out of their own accord in manic response, driving me up toward the head of the bed, and pulling part way off him. I cried out and wrapped my legs around his waist, arching, jerking to pull him into me again. He let himself down onto his elbows and started pumping into me, long hard deep strokes, his mouth clamping onto the side of my chest and sucking near that overly sensitive spot in time with his thrusts.

He slowed his thrusts, trying to control himself, and I didn't react to the difference. He stopped sucking and I relaxed all over at once, the orgasm immediately becoming less extreme, starting to fade. After a moment more of slow thrusting, he grabbed onto a nipple with his lips, and, setting his teeth around the bottom, started to tug on it, playfully, like a puppy.

This set me off again, but a slow building, and he stiffened, holding himself very still as my insides started to ripple again. But he wasn't able to hold back anymore; everything was bubbling up and over, I could hear it in his voice as he again begged, soft voiced and quivering. "Please? I can't...."

Somehow I heard it, and understood; when I nodded, he started in again with long full strokes, sucking and nibbling on my nipple, lightly stroking that spot under my arm.

I shrieked in his ear and threw my arms around him, desperately trying to ride out my own wildness. My cunt spasmed in time with our strokes, and he started to come, pounding into me with a force that surprised both of us. One stroke, two, and I felt the difference, felt him swelling inside me, his cock leaping with the power that's thrusting through both of us. I grabbed his head and dragged him down for a kiss as he three, four and five came, alive, deep inside me, lifting me off the bed with the force of his orgasm, another orgasm over-cresting mine, like a larger ocean wave. All my senses were subsumed and this was the only stimulus; my ears roared with my blood as we were suspended together, falling over the brink.

Sometime later, a separation of bodies. Sometime later, a finding of words.

"Did I do well, my Lady?"

"Yes, rather. Was that what you needed?"

"Yes. More than I ever knew."

SLEEPING NAKED
by Thomas S. Roche

Sherry's not so good with clothes. Maybe it comes from being a Florida girl. Around the house, she's always naked, from the moment she walks in the door in the evening to the time she steps out of the shower in the morning. She gardens in the backyard nude except for a pair of running shoes or, on hot days, a pair of 99-cent flip-flops, unconcerned about the crack in the fence or the sleazy neighbor who suns on his roof nearby.

When we have guests coming over—whether it's the landlord, her best friend or the pizza boy—Sherry pouts for a moment, inconsolable over the fact that she has to put on clothes to receive them. The clothes she dons are as limited in scope as possible—shorts or sweats with no panties, tank top or T-shirt with no bra.

The second we're alone again, her clothes are scattered in piles around the floor. I know from experience that her exhibitionist streak means she'd rather just greet the mailman or the cable guy naked, and it's only through some incongruous fragment of propriety that she manages to put on any clothes at all.

In bed, the coldest days find her stretched out nude under piles of blankets, her slender limbs shivering and her pale flesh a field of goosebumps for the first fifteen minutes despite the incursion of the electric blanket and the space heater. If I get into bed with clothes on, she claws them off of me, craving the touch of my flesh on hers. I quit arguing months ago, since when she strips me she never fails to put her money where her mouth is—or, more accurately, her mouth right where her highly active libido is.

This January night, though, turns out to be the rare exception to her many rules of nudity. She's been traveling for the holidays, visiting friends in her home state, and before I left to pick her up at the airport I neglected to turn on the heater and the electric blanket. She hates traveling, and it exhausts her, so her bitchy dismay turns to bitchy fatigue within moments of walking in to the freezing-cold apartment. I watch as she strips out of her travel clothes and wriggles her naked body into a set of long underwear, tight cream-colored silk hugging her slim ass, her nipples so hard it hurts me to look at them poking through the wicking fabric where her small breasts distend it.

"I'm going to stay up and study for a while," I tell her.

"Bullshit you are," she says, clutching the comforter to her neck as if its proximity will lock in the slowly-building heat of the electric blanket. "You forgot to turn on the blanket, so you're my bed warmer. Get in here."

I shrug, strip off my clothes, and pull back the covers. She grabs them with a wild-eyed look of terror on her face.

"No!" She looks at me suspiciously. "What the fuck are you doing naked?"

"Not everyone comes from the Sun Belt."

I manage to squeeze my way under the covers without disrupting her perceived bubble of insulation, and once I'm there, she wrestles them over me, enclosing me as best she can. She wraps her arms and legs around me.

"You're freezing," she says, her voice a mélange of shivers and Southern decadence. "I forgot I fucking live in Alaska," she drawls with a disgruntled snap, shivering as she squirms her way under the covers.

"San Francisco," I say. "But close."

"It may as well be Alaska," she says. "It's fucking freezing."

"I think it's nice and warm," I say, just to annoy her.

"Say that again. I dare you."

She cuddles up against me, her entire body quivering with cold. I reach out and pick up my text book, turning to Chapter 23, thermodynamics.

"Glad to be home?" I ask her.

"Wake me when it's June."

She shivers against me, her cheek pressed against my belly as I sit propped up in bed trying to understand the fine points of heat distribution. She's all but buried under the covers, whimpering pathetically as she squirms about seeking the nonexistent warm spots in the bed. Within minutes, though, her exhaustion takes over—she never could sleep on planes.

"Sherry?" I ask her.

No response. She's already long gone into the land of Morpheus, a land where, hopefully, the sun shines on her naked flesh as she stretches out on steaming patches of volcanic rock.

The space heater blows hot air at me. I've never had the hot-blooded streak that Sherry does; I like it cold. I long ago learned to accept the fine sheen of sweat that forms on me whenever Sherry and I are together; it's a small price to pay. A simple law of thermodynamics, as my textbook keeps telling me. Or maybe that law was in different book. Still, it's hard to keep my mind on my studies as Sherry's sleeping body slowly warms up.

Gradually, I feel the uncomfortable drip of sweat on my legs. I prefer goosebumps, but I'm not about to shift my body and risk upsetting the perfect balance that allowed my girlfriend to fall asleep despite the chill of the apartment. Instead, I stick one leg out and feel the welcome cooling of the air on my moistened flesh. I lose myself in my book, only noticing in small increments that the room is getting warmer.

Sherry's getting warmer, too, as her breathing grows soft and steady. She clutches herself to me, seeking the warmth of my body to augment the ever-encroaching heat of the electric blanket. Her arm drapes over my lap and nuzzles my naked cock; I feel it hardening partway. A restless sleeper, she writhes in slumber, inching away from me as the bed gets warmer. My cock goes back to its disinterested state as I descend into thermodynamics, making swift progress through the chapter.

I lose track of time, and an hour or so later when I set down the book and stretch, Sherry has squirmed partway out of the covers. What's more, she's sleepily tugged her silk long underwear up over her belly.

I watch her sleeping as she curls into a ball facing me and writhes, her hands clutching somnolently at the hem of the shirt. It comes up over her breasts, revealing her nipples still hard with chill, pierced by bright silver rings.

I say her name, but get no response. She's doing a strip-tease for me in her sleep. Her need to be naked is greater than her need for warmth—and besides, the bedroom's getting pretty warm.

I wonder how far my sleeping stripper will take it.

I get my answer, or the first part of it, a moment later when she utters a fitful sigh and claws at the top again with one hand, pulling it up over her other arm, half doffing the thermal shirt.

My cock is immediately hard, drinking in the lush beauty of those tits I've missed so much, even as a shimmer of goosebumps goes across them. I reach out and pull down the covers a little, hoping the room is now warm enough that my scandalous exploitation won't wake her. She starts to wriggle, and in another instant her shirt comes over her head, revealing her upper body even as it shrouds her face.

I reach out and tug at the hem of the shirt, pulling it over her head. It comes free with a pop, and I gently slide it over her arms, revealing Sherry's upper body.

I say her name again, but get no response. I wonder if there's a name for this— it's not quite sleepwalking, but close. Sleep-stripping?

I get out of bed, go to the hall closet, and dig out a second space heater. I prop it up at the foot of the bed and turn it on full, then climb back under the covers, rubbing my hands together rapidly to warm them before I put my hand on her back and gently stroke it. She responds with a sleepy sigh, lifting her ass slightly, which is when I realize she's pulled the waist of her thermal underwear all the way down to the curve in her ass. When she rolls on her side and tosses the covers back, the pale tuft of her pubic hair is just visible at the top of the cream-colored silk. She claws at her pants ineffectually, obviously wanting to get rid of the bottoms but unable to achieve the coordination in her lethargic state.

So I lend her a hand. I peel back the covers and tug at her long underwear, pulling it down until it slides off her ass. Now her pussy is visible, and its faint smell makes my cock get hard all the way.

I disappear under the covers, careful to pull them all the way over her. Curling up against her legs, I immerse myself in the heat of the bed, stifling with the electric blanket on full. I work my hands under the elastic of Sherry's long johns, pulling them down her thighs.

It takes some doing to get them over her knees and down her calves without waking her, but I manage it. When the elastic cuffs come over her ankles, I ease her legs open and push the covers up to make sure she's still swathed in warmth.

Deep in the darkness, all I can smell is her pussy. I don't even know if she's still asleep, and I don't care. I find her cunt with my mouth and gently draw my tongue up the length of her slit, teasing her open. I hear a faint moan above me, sleepy or aroused, I can't tell.

But her pussy is wet—dripping. It tastes strong, as if for an entire day of weather delays, departure lounges and holding patterns, she was thinking about getting fucked.

My tongue descends on her clit and I begin to suck, gently at first, then more fervently as my cock pushes painfully against the flannel sheets. I slide my hands, warm from rubbing, under her ass and lift her to me, licking from cunt to clit and back again. Then I focus on her clit, licking harder and faster as I strain my hard cock into the soft sheets. I hear her moaning.

Awake or asleep? Unimportant—she's warm.

I lick my way up her belly, sliding my body on top of her. I pause at her tits and take each nipple in my mouth, warming them with my tongue but doing little to alleviate how hard they are. When my face reaches Sherry's, her eyes are open, looking up at me with hunger.

My mouth plunges onto hers and our tongues entwine as my cock nuzzles against her opening. She lifts her hips and pushes me into her, and I thrust deep in a single fluid motion, my arms extended so I can tuck my hands under her and grip her ass. She whimpers suddenly as my cock reaches its deepest point inside her, and then she grinds her hips up toward me, forcing my cock harder against the walls of her pussy. Her arms snake around my body and she pulls me firmly onto her, her thrusts matching mine as we kiss. Sweat pools between us as our hips pound together, each violent thrust coaxing heat from the bond between us.

When I sense she's close to coming, I grab her hair and pull her head back so I can bite her neck, drawing a groan from her lips as I give her a hickey that would scandalize the hell out of her Florida friends. I drive into her harder and she comes, her pussy clenching fiercely around my shaft and her nails digging furrows into my sweat-slick flesh. She climaxes a second time before I let myself go within her pussy, my come heating her from the inside. She clutches me close and nuzzles my neck.

"You said to wake you up when it got warm," I say, feeling a little guilty for ravaging a sleeping girlfriend.

"You waited until it was hot," she says, running her hands up her sides where our bodies press together, rivulets of moisture dribbling out. "But then, you're the expert in thermodynamics."

I press my mouth to hers and grind my half-hard cock inside her, bringing another moan, this one muffled, from her warm lips.

UTTERLY NUDE
by Maxim Jakubowski

He'd always been attracted, sometimes fascinated by the smooth hairless crotches of women. Not just the fact that some women wished to shave their sexual parts, or more likely in the pursuit of fashion, wax them. What also exercised his imagination were the deep-set motivations behind the decision to reveal their cunts so openly, to regress to a state of far from innocent childhood, unprotected by a bush of curls or a minor forest of imitation barbed wire in all shades of colors and textures. Quite often, he had convinced a lover to allow him to trim her pubic hair and, one occasion, to actually allow him to shave her fully. The experience itself had proven most erotic and the ensuing fucking had acquired an extra dimension. It was summer and the South of France and, the next day, he had half jokingly suggested she refrain from wearing her thong under her short skirt when they went out dining and she had playfully agreed. A memory that lingered with him much longer than the intensity of their love-making. But she had drawn the line at returning to that nude beach some miles away from the port where they were staying with her cunt in full naked display. He had failed to persuade her to do so, and his innocent request had visibly irritated her. It would seem that a hairless cunt was a private matter that should only be witnessed by a lover of long standing. By coincidence or otherwise, this was to be their last trip together.

His next mistress was already shaven. Had been so for years, long before he emerged on her scene. It seems the practice was widespread amongst young women in Germany, and having noted the fact during endless telephone conversations and e-mail exchanges, this was one aspect of hers that had immediately attracted him to her in the first place. And her jovial willingness to sleep with him. Undressing her for the first time, in a hotel room in Frankfurt that smelled of illicit sex already, proved an exhilarating experience, but also a sort of anti-climax as he finally unveiled the silky smoothness of her cunt, and the red gash of her sexual parting in a wet state of readiness. The thought briefly occurred to him that it would have been so much more exciting to have witnessed her passage from hairiness to utter nudity himself. Maybe it wasn't the state of nakedness of a mons veneris that did these strange things to him, but the very act of revelation, the passage from hirsute parts to billiard-ball shininess. He hadn't had much time to reflect on things though with her, as he quickly discovered the ever so slightly masochistic streak that illuminated the young woman's sexuality, as she greedily invited him to twist her nipples between the vice of her abandoned hairpins once he had set her dark auburn hair loose.

"Yes," she had moaned, begging for the pain.

He had soon forgotten the initial ecstatic vision of her smooth cunt as further excesses quickly suggested themselves to him, none of which she rejected during the course of a long night of sheer, mutual madness.

But the fascination remained. Encouraged, exacerbated, provoked, kept alive by the torrent of images of exposed, naked cunts he kept on coming across in magazines, books and even movies (Europeans ones by Peter Greenaway, Julio Medem, Mike Figgis and others...).

So, it was no surprise that one summer whilst on holidays

on a small Caribbean island, his enfevered mind should spin an unlikely variation on the theme. This was not a place where nudity was tolerated on beaches, despite the idyllic setting that so effortlessly evoked the Garden of Eden and its bucolic innocence. Even topless displays of female pulchritude were few and far between here. The heat over his first few days at the resort had proven oppressive, steamy, sticky, with no relief in sight. On previous trips here, he had been close to the hurricane season and there had always been a gentle wind rising over the ocean from mid to late morning to cool one's body down. By lunchtime, every day, he was sweating profusely and his trunks or shorts stuck aggressively to his skin, the friction between the material and his flesh annoying and increasingly unpleasant. Dredging up instant nostalgia and longing for those nude beaches in France he had frequented some years back.

Maybe he should shave. Like a woman. It might feel cooler, he thought. And then remembered how some past conquest had once mentioned how unpleasant it could become when the hair inevitably grew back, the skin irritable and prone to bursting out in unseemly bumps. He would chose cream. It should be safe if women used it under their arms, he reckoned. He located some in the hotel's lobby shop and deciphered the instructions in Spanish as best he could....

Straight from the tube he squeezed out the thick white paste that smelled of almond oil in parallel trails across his thick, dark curls and flattened and liberally spread the viscous substance until his bush was fully obscured and covered. The label said to leave it soak in for five minutes, although to take care not to rub it in and especially not to exceed ten minutes. He kept an eye on his watch. Then, with the help of the green plastic spatula supplied in the depilating cream's pack, he began gently rubbing the drying cream away. It worked. The hair was coming of with a minimum of effort. He sat on the edge of the bath tub, his legs spread open and began to systematically scrape away the dead vegetation surrounding his now half-erect penis until the whole area looked uncannily bare, the paler than pale skin a mighty contrast with the onset of a deep tan across the rest of his body. After rinsing the newly depilated zone with some warm water, he passed his fingers over the whole area and found it surprisingly, pleasantly silky. Which conjured instant memories of the cunts of the women he had caressed lustfully during the course of recent sexual encounters. His hand moved down to his cock, and he was taken back by the fact that some stray, almost spiky hairs still adorned the lower reaches of the thickening trunk of his member. His fingers lowered and swept across his testicles and again became aware of the sprinkling of hairs that coated them. Out came the cream again and he covered his balls all the way down to his perineum, as well as the stem of his cock. Soon, he was totally bare, all the way from his lower stomach area to his anal opening.

It felt good. Curiously arousing and it proved difficult during those few first days of total nudity not to touch and finger himself constantly. As if the skin above his jutting cock had acquired a new, sensual texture and the taut sack of his balls invited the tentative contact of errant fingertips as he explored the newly uncovered territory. He imagined how a woman's tongue would taste him, lick him and again came hard in the wink of an eye.

At regular interval, he would examine his genitals in the mirror of the bathroom, or the half mirror that the hotel provided in the bedroom. He became an inveterate voyeur of his own parts, finding new subtleties in the ever-changing shades of white and pale brown in the virgin skin that dominated his cock, the reddish hue of his heavy balls. Actually, his cock now appeared longer, thicker, bigger, not that he'd ever had grounds for complaint previously. There was a nagging desire to expose himself, to surprise others, to reveal to the world at large how utter his nudity now was. He even began to dispense with underwear altogether, dangling loose under his trousers and shorts in the resort's large dining room that overlooked the sea, joyous with the secret knowledge of his uncommon state under the already thin material. It was definitely most arousing. One morning, he even deliberately left the room around five in the morning and walked a few miles up the beach to an area he had once spotted, far from the hotels and beach guards, and swam naked. More than naked. The lapping of the water against his parts was joyous, liberating, even stronger than the feeling he had experienced the first time he had swam on a nude beach, albeit with his previous abundance of pubic air. It wasn't just the sexual effect of his newly acquired nudity but a weird sense of possibilities that engulfed his brain.

He thought he now understood why some women depilated their sexual areas. He sympathized. Empathized. This was more than mere hygiene or practicality. To the extent that the compulsive desire to present himself in total submission, in all his childlike nudity, began to dominate his dreams. Surely there was no greater sense of vulnerability to be displayed thus, so shorn of all protection, sexually available to all comers and potential users. For the first time, he was beginning to understand better the mind frame of submissive women, all those doughty heroines from O to the legions of abused women from the Roquelaure tales of Anne Rice and her cohorts of more recent followers. He could close his eyes and silently yearn to be tied to some pole or tree, legs held apart by a spreader bar, ridiculous cock dangling in the forest breeze, while men of all shapes, sizes and sexual persuasions could liberally gaze at him, touch his parts, weigh their melancholy nudity in the palm of their hands, poke his holes, gently slap his butt cheeks, examine his teeth as he lay in wait to be auctioned. Yes, knowing how unprotected he was down there literally made him feel like a sexual slave in waiting. He did have a roaring imagination, he surely did.

Back in Europe, he would often wake at night from savage dreams of exotic, novelistic adventures full of rape and heavy use by Masters. His lust raged at the idea of such ravishment and in each scene or sequence that his fever lust conjured, there were also beautiful women watching as he was being defiled, all with Mona Lisa smiles, some clothed in sheer silk, others in progressive stages of deshabille, calmly appreciating the sheer art his torturers exercised as they took merciless advantage of his now so prominent cock and shiny balls, and induced endless after endless erections until he felt he was about to burst, as each toy, object or alien penis dug its painful way into his innards, stretching him more than he ever thought possible, deep-throating him until he gagged, and all because his shaven parts betrayed his abject condition as a sexual slave available to all, obedient, displayed, ripe for defilement.

He even went so far as advertising himself in veiled terms as a sub for use when he ventured onto Internet chat rooms, hoping for takers and resolute enough to follow through should someone local and reasonably dominant actually take him up on the offer. But no one did; all they sought were female subs, no doubt similarly shaven. His sisters in arm.

And, at four or so in the morning when the dreams came to their spectacular climax (you couldn't call them nightmares after all), he would invariably be untied, his collar straightened and a chain attached to it and he was led, so naked and proud, to a stone table where the spread-eagled body of the most beautiful young blonde he had ever dreamed of was on public display to the leering gaze of a growing crowd, and, as a reward for having survived his own ordeal, he would be summoned to mount her, required to perform, take her virginity. And always he would note that she also had been depilated, her cunt lips gaping open like flowers and the skin surrounding her gash slippery like glass, smooth as a window pane, and when their flesh made contact, it would be like an electric shock. Nakedness touching nudity, as obscene as two skeletons mating, the nec plus ultra of performance art. At which stage, he usually woke up, his cock hard and raging and ready to spill, like the lone tree in a defoliated forest.

But the first time after the Caribbean holiday that he took a woman to bed, she barely noticed the uncommon hairlessness of his crotch, didn't even remark upon it. Which not only brought him down to earth but also made him temporarily impotent. They parted in embarrassment. Anyway, he reflected, following her departure, she had just been trimmed and the conjugation of his cock and her cunt would have certainly lacked the obligatory magic. From here onwards, he swore to himself, he would only have sex with women who were similarly, utterly nude. Somehow, it became a clever, subtle question he would manage to introduce into the proceedings of seduction from an early stage. Some minded and went their own way; others were coy, some intrigued, partly offended by his outrageous and indecent curiosity about the state of their parts. He was not a totally hopeless case and still practiced the art of courting with a modicum of elegance and intelligence and did not find it impossible to convince an attractive woman to go to bed with him, but he invariably became the one to surprise and disappoint them shortly after their answers to his one track enquiries always seemed to reveal their uselessness to him. It was not so much that he didn't feel capable of convincing them, once lovers or in a bedroom, naked, lustful, to allow him to shave them; no, he wanted them to come to him in a natural state of nudity below from the outset, like Venus arising from the shell, their cunt more naked than naked ready for his kiss, his tongue, the heat of his lips. He had no wish for preliminaries, or hard work. Once together, they must both shed their clothing and witness their bare areas meeting, like waves lapping the shore, like a pagan ritual.

But somehow all the women he came across socially or attempted to weave into the fabric of his life now guarded the sanctity of their pubic hair like dragons, and bristled at his unkind suggestion they should do away with their heavenly bush.

So, instead, he masturbated a lot, familiarizing himself even better with the new texture and feel of his own cock and balls. Altogether a pitiful state of affairs for a man who had now reached the stage where he was actually turning women away. And the fact he so often would not take advantage of their proffered charms—he would never say exactly why—only spurred them to attack him with more zest. Never had he been more popular with women, and never had he not fucked anyone for such a long period of sexual drought. If only they knew, he thought, as he perused a room full of beauty and talent. But then he couldn't just drop his trousers here and now and expose himself and reveal his secret. Or should he?

But he was a patient man. One day, she would arrive, he was convinced, and at the very moment that bare cock and bare cunt would meet, as the mushroom tip of his thick purple cock would at last breach her opening and plunge deep into her pinkness, then their sex flesh would finally meet with a vengeance. Smoothness to smoothness, silk against silk, electrons against electrons, blissful innocence against total vulnerability. And everything would explode in an orgy of momentous pleasure, like an atomic bomb exploding. Like the end of the world.

Until then, he would wait, he reckoned. And stay chaste, and shaven.

WHAT DO YOU SAY TO A NAKED LADY?
by Wiley Smith

It's not every day that you see a naked lady lounging on a float in the middle of a deserted lake. All right, so this lake wasn't really a lake, but a man-made pond. And it wasn't completely deserted, but right off the Point Reyes/Petaluma Road, shrouded only slightly by a row of skinny green trees.

But it *was* deserted enough.

And lake *enough*.

And she was *definitely* naked enough.

I've driven this road about a thousand times on my way to and from work, and I've gazed into the deep green-blue of the water and seen the deserted float and wondered what it might be like to sneak out there for a quick dip and a sunbathe. In a moment of weakness, I even confessed the fantasy to a buddy of mine over a beer one night, describing the place as a mini-oasis between work and home.

"You're crazy," Liam told me. "You'd be arrested in a heartbeat. You know how many cops cruise that strip looking for speeders?"

I shrugged.

"It would be their great joy and pleasure to write you up for public indecency."

"I don't think anyone would notice me," I said. "If you suddenly showed up there out of nowhere, people would assume it was your own property. Who would guess that you were some crazy naked interloper?"

Liam shrugged. "Seems risky." And then he drained half the beer and grinned his shark smile at me. "Too risky for you, man. You'd never do it."

I didn't respond. I just thought to myself, *"Is that a dare?"*

Maybe that's what this girl was up to, I thought. Or maybe she really *did* own the place and was simply basking in her own not-so-private wonderland. Whatever she was doing, once I saw her in all of her glory, I couldn't get her out of my mind. Ten miles down the road, I swung an illegal U-turn and quickly headed back in her direction.

I knew there was a chance that she'd be gone by the time I reached the lake. Perhaps I'd hallucinated her in my driving-induced oasis, conjuring up an image of a feline female who was exactly my type. The thing was, I had to find out for certain, so I parked my car on the opposite side of the road in a dirt-crusted pull out, and headed down the slope toward the lake.

She was still there. Right there in the center of the float, just as naked as she had been before. I saw the spread of her ginger-colored hair and the warm tan polished look of her skin, and I took a breath and kept on walking. I didn't see any "no-trespassers" sign nearby. I could claim that I'd...that I'd *what*? Gotten a flat? She could easily hike up to the ridge and see that I hadn't. But would she hike in the nude just to be sure? That was the question.

But there was an even bigger question in my mind as I stepped to the side of the lake. I didn't have any sort of opening line prepared, and I'd never been in this particular type of situation before. I mean, really: What do you say to a naked lady?

I cleared my throat, but she didn't even look my way. I kicked the dirt a bit, then cleared my throat again. Finally, for want of anything better to say, I called out, "Hey!"

For a moment, she didn't move. Then she slowly lifted

her head up and gazed at me. The look in her eyes would have told me what I needed to know—if I could have seen her eyes. But they were covered by sleek mirrored shades, and I didn't have a clue. Was she glaring? Or frightened? Or ashamed? Or....

"The water's lovely," she said. "Want to take a dip?"

Yes, I did. In the water. In *her* waters to be more precise.

"You're Jamie, aren't you?" she said next, and that's when I realized I knew her. Christ, what an idiot I was. So captivated was I by her gorgeous naked body and her insolence at being naked in broad vision of any passing vehicle, that I hadn't realized she was a friend of my neighbor's—that I'd seen both stunning women sunbathe plenty of times in our backyard. Not quite naked in their itsy string bikinis, but naked enough. Naked enough so that when Liam asked me why I'd never gotten the nerve to ask her out, I'd challenged him with, "Well, what would you say to a naked lady?"

"Is this yours?" I asked, spreading my arms to indicate the lake and the land around.

She shook her head, and now I did see a blush. At least, I thought so.

"I just drive by every day," she said, "and I've always wanted to take a dip. And today, I just thought, *What the fuck?* You know what I mean?"

I nodded, gravely. I knew. She really was the girl of my fucking dreams. Literally.

"So you're coming in?"

I kicked off my boots and started on my jeans. She took my actions as a positive answer, and then slid her sunglasses up on her hair, smiling at me appreciatively. I moved into the water without thinking. No repercussions. No worries. Just me in the water, swimming quickly to the float and pulling myself out at her side.

When I got there, I realized that I was once again without

words. Luckily for me, I didn't need any. The girl had plenty of them on her own.

"You took awhile."

I stared at her quizzically. At least, I hoped that's how I stared at her. Mostly, I was so taken by her lovely heart-shaped face and her drop-dead beautiful body, I was doing my best to hide my state of total arousal. This was completely impossible, of course, since I was now as naked as she was. But I hoped I looked deeply interested in what she had to say, and not only interested in jumping her.

"Usually, Cat says you're home by this time."

"You knew my travel plans," I guessed, knowing I was correct even as I said the words.

"I knew your fantasy," she told me.

I shook my head. *She* was my fantasy. Dipping in the water was a mere daydream.

"How?" I asked next.

"Your friend, Liam? He said he was sick of you not taking the first step, so he told Cat you liked me. And I've been interested in you all summer, so I thought I'd make something happen."

"You have?" I asked.

"You think I'd parade around in that bathing suit if I didn't want you looking? God, the thing is just a little bit of floss wrapped around three tiny triangles."

I just stared at her, dumbfounded. I don't know anything about women. That was suddenly clear to me. She'd *wanted* me to watch her? If I'd realized that before, I would have approached her way the hell back in June. Maybe my summer wouldn't have been quite so lonely.

"Cat let me know when you get home each day. I figured out the rest."

"You said something about a fantasy..."

"Liam mentioned that you daydream a lot on this road."

"Yeah," I said, remembering the description over the barbecue. Remembering Liam's ridicule. "I didn't say anything about hooking up with someone on a raft, though."

"That was my own guess," she said, coming into my arms and kissing me. "I thought we might have the same sort of feelings about this place."

I was warming up to the fact that we were just talking together—naked and natural—as if talking in the middle of this lake was the most normal thing in the world. And then she moved closer and slid into my arms, and suddenly the concept of making love was even more natural than talking. The way her body fit with mine, as I'd known it would, still managed to blow me away.

She took charge, pushing me onto my back and looking down at me with the most delicious sort of half-smile.

"Ready?"

I nodded and let her climb astride me, working her hips up and back as she began to ride my cock. She was uninhibited, as I might have guessed from the fact that she'd been sunbathing naked in a lake easily seen by every passing vehicle. But now that she was on my body, the trait appealed to me even more. She moved slowly and languidly, at first, almost echoing the rhythm of the water lapping at the float. Then she speeded up, and I had to catch my breath as the power of her heat flooded over me.

I trailed my fingers along her collarbones and down her chest. I touched her sweet round nipples and she arched her back and moaned. I pinched her nipples harder between my thumbs and forefingers, and her moans grew more intense, deeper in pitch. I liked the way she sounded, and the way she looked, all flushed and hot in the sun and from our movements, glazed with sweat as if gilded. She was in control of her movements, the way she rocked me, but at the same time, she didn't seem to mind losing control to pleasure.

I slid one hand down her body and tapped my fingertips against her clit. Her eyes opened and she gazed right at me, lips parted, nodding gently so that I knew to keep up what I was doing. With each light touch of my fingertips on her clit, she squeezed me, and I could hardly believe how amazing it felt. There we were, in the midst of nature, in the center of a lake, while right off the well-trafficked road. We were alone, yet outside, and I almost had to shake myself to make sure that *this* wasn't my mirage. That this was real.

But then she said my name again, and I knew this was no oasis. "Jamie," she purred. "Oh, god that feels good."

She was wild, all right, wild and so fucking beautiful, and when she came, it was as if I saw fire in her eyes. I rode her out, a few seconds later, bucking into her, fucking her so hard that the float moved ferociously in the water, rocking with us. I can't remember a time that ever felt that good. Not with anyone else. Not ever.

She slid off me and into my arms, and I held onto her tight, her skin so warm and slippery, her hair long and free. She'd planned this. With the help of Liam and Cat. She'd planned this and I couldn't get over that fact. But then, looking down at her, I thought of something. "What was your concept," I couldn't help but ask, "if someone else found you out here?"

"Found me?"

"You know, found you before I did?"

"I was banking on the fact that nobody would disturb me," she grinned. "I mean, I thought anyone who caught sight of me would be too shell-shocked to know what to do. You know, what would *you* say to a naked lady?"

I smiled back at her. "I can't think of one single thing," I said. "Not to say, anyway. But I can think of a *world* of things I'd like to do—"

STRIPPING JANICE
by Eden Baltulis

I watch her through the slit in the curtain; she is unaware of my presence and the shut window allows no sound to give away my movement.

We've done this before. Like a pining teenager I go to her house and stand on the outside, looking up at her, watching her move. She knows I'm there; she has to. Why else does she make such a show of her undressing? Why else does she just happen to leave the curtain open every night?

In her room of gold, she walks from dresser to bed and back again. She is putting on her clothes, covering up her beautiful skin that's pale as moonstone. She doesn't wear panties, hasn't in the months I've known her. Black pants go on first, shiny, probably satin because the light catches on them and highlights her every curve. The bra she removes from her dresser is so white it blinds me in the gloom. There's no delicate material here, no lace, no ribbons or bows or tiny seashell-pink roses. It's just expansive white, over her breasts, trapping them underneath and making her flatter than before in a degree that's barely noticeable.

From her closet she takes a jacket and it slides over her skin as I imagine my hand would, smoothly, imperceptibly light and warm. She glances in the mirror, adjusts a strand of hair that has escaped from her ponytail, and leaves the room. I am moving to the front of the house, watching her get into her car and drive away.

She's always leaving me, the lady with the alabaster flesh.

*****

The next week I am at her house again; this time I've been invited in. Like the old friends we are, we sit in the living room, sip tea and avoid eye contact—she because my stare unnerves her, I, because if I were to look into her eyes, I would want to kiss her and after all we've been through, a kiss now would be impolite. We had our break-up sex a long time ago.

"Ayesha," she begins, but her voice fades near the end and she grows silent. I look at her knees and see the slight redness to them, as if she's been scrubbing floors like a maid. I put down my teacup and notice that, in relation to her, my skin is not as lovely. My skin is worn, tanned by the sun and many afternoons outside. My hands are cold, blue-tinted. I know her skin is always white as milk, except between her thighs, but I cannot think of that now. Not now. We're trying to be proper and avoid the past, and once again I'm giving in to her beauty and cannot help myself from remembering.

"Ayesha, I know you're outside at night. I see you. Your eyes gleam in the darkness when you watch me, like there's some phosphorescence inside."

Her voice is low and harsh, broken from too many cigarettes. I imagine her throat looks like sandpaper, feels like steel wool. I'm glad the rest of her was never so abrasive.

"Are you even listening?"

I jump at the sudden sound of her voice and look guiltily at her. "No, I was thinking about you, us—"

"There's a reason it didn't last. You were too wrapped up in the superficial aspects of me. You loved my skin, but not my heart. You loved me on the outside and even though I was cruel to you and withered on the inside, you stayed. I could not go on taking advantage of someone who had no clue they were being used."

I hear her, but don't respond. With my eyes, I'm removing her shirt, letting the soft material move with gravity and flow over her collarbones like water, catching on the swell of her breasts, covering her nipples like a barely-there censored sign.

She rises and comes towards me. I look up, catch her eye, and it's there, all our history, right there in the forest shade of her iris, imprinted like DNA onto her very soul. The message moves into my brain: she misses me.

"Things cannot continue," she speaks the words her mind tells her to keep inside, "no more can you come stand in my garden and watch me. No more..." I'm gone again, admiring her feet and their creamy color in contrast to her black heels, when she brings her hand against my face, softly, with the threat that it could be done harder.

"Ayesha! For Christ's sake pay attention. This is it. After today I want nothing to do with you, and you cannot keep following me, stalking me. You must go on...honey, it's been five months. We will not mend what was broken, we will not have a second chance. Exes are exes for a reason." Her hand caresses my face and I find myself unconsciously licking one of her fingers. It's smooth as sea glass and vaguely salty, like it always was.

"Janice, I love your skin. I need to see it, feel it, have it near me. No one I've met has skin like yours, so white it could be translucent, so soft it doesn't feel like that of a thirty-plus woman. Please, just undress for me one more time, and I'll never stand outside your window again. Janice, I swear."

She looks at me pityingly. She knows she is my weakness and finds me less a person because of it. But if she only knew how beautiful she was.

"One more night, Ayesha, then never again. After tonight, don't stop here."

I'm listening now, and tears are in my eyes as she speaks. She is right, I know this, but I cannot think of the day when never again shall I caress her, touching the smoothness of her arms, and the curve of her belly. I will myself to put the future away and think about the present. We have another night. I have hours to be near her. That is all that matters.

I am to return later. She tells me to go eat and so I do, sitting in the restaurant, mentally undressing the other people, finding them all lacking when compared to her. Janice told me to return at nine-thirty, and I watch the clock move in a slow revolution to that time.

Then I go back.

When she opens the door, it's like the light returning to my life, until I see what she's wearing. Curse her, the bitch! She knows of my lust for her undressed skin and has taken every precaution to ensure she is completely covered up.

"Janice, you look very untouchable."

Her eyes smile. They are the only part of her that I can see. She speaks, and her voice is less articulate that it had been earlier in the day, likely due to the leather mask on her face. "Come in."

I step into her house, feeling betrayed and unwelcome. When the door shuts behind me, it's like the lid of a coffin slamming home—permanent. I swallow hard, and pray my nervousness won't ruin this evening, this last chance.

Silently she leads the way through her house. Not much has changed since I've last been in it. The bedroom is still in the same place, the same faded photographs on the door. I look for my picture among the faces there but don't see it. She must have removed me in more than one sense.

We enter her bedroom, the room I've been in so many times before under such better circumstances. Lingerie and bondage gear hang from hooks placed in the walls, painful reminders of when I last saw her in (or out) of them.

In the center of the room is a chair with chains attached.

Her bed is unmade and in a corner. That's different since last I was there. The hair on the back of my neck prickles when I realize she's standing right behind me.

"You should sit down." It is more of a command than a suggestion.

I tilt my head back and catch her eye. She's staring at me, as if this entire night depends on whether or not I listen to her. I give her a half-smile, wary, and go sit down.

Janice stands in front of me. It's only now in the harsh florescent light of her steel-and-glass bedroom do I notice the full extent of her outfit. It's like armor.

Black heeled leather boots encase her feet and legs. Darkness covers her torso. I can't even see her hands; they too are enclosed in shiny black. Even her hair is hidden away, and her mouth and nose are small bulges under the face mask. I wonder how well she can breathe. I wonder if she's enjoying this, knowing how much I want to see her naked.

She just stands there. I squirm uncomfortably then sit still, thinking. Does she actually like wearing that thing or is she just putting up with it as she knows how much the outfit torments me? Is it shiny on the inside? Is it warm and soft to touch, or slippery and cool? Is it easy to remove? I reach my hand out to touch her thigh and a gloved hand smacks mine away.

"No touching," she says.

Janice, oh the torment you cause! Is this your form of punishment? First, I cannot gaze at your skin, and now I cannot even touch you through a barrier. What fun last night will this be? My sentiment must show in my face because she moves close to me and I can smell the perfume she wears, the same kind as when we were dating, with overtones of a delicate womanly scent.

She's within a foot of me, my face level with her stomach. I can feel the heat that radiates off her. Unconsciously, my hand rises from the armrest and with the lightest of touches, brushes against her lower thigh.

My hand hasn't even returned to its original position when she grabs it. "I said 'don't touch'! You never were one to listen." A chain gets wrapped around my wrist, then around my other, crossing in front of me like a barrier at a carnival ride. *Please keep all body parts inside the vehicle.* Her eyes seem very bright behind her mask as she clamps me down into the chair. I try and wiggle my hands; they are motionless. Janice notices this attempt and smiles. "Now that I have your full attention…"

In the light that never ceases to reminds me of a hospital hallway she stands triumphant before me. Once my lady, now nothing more than a friend wishing I'd stop hanging around so much, she embodies everything I ever wanted, ever will desire. I know that never again will I be able to call her mine.

She removes the mask. There is a heavy zipper at the back and in the silence the sound of it being opened is almost too loud, too crass. Her chestnut hair flows onto her shoulders, a picture of freedom in a frame of restraint, and her mouth widens into a smile.

She's enjoying this, this control game, this teasing. Loathed as I am to admit it, so am I. The anticipation of watching her remove the clothing piece by piece is almost too much to bear. I realize that between my legs I am wet, and I wonder if she'll notice.

Next off are her gloves. She knows how much I love her hands, and hungrily I watch her peel off the blackness that looks like wet seaweed from her elegant hands, the hands of a pianist, which as we both know are also well suited for other pleasures. She's painted her nails silver; they look like small mirrors, and as she drops the gloves to the floor I see my face reflected in her nails, tiny, distorted and eager. I'm ashamed to know how obvious it is that I want her. I look away.

She grabs my chin and makes me look at her, into her eyes. "You wanted this, Ayesha, you wanted to watch, to see my skin, to see me naked, so look. Look!" Letting go of me she steps back and unclasps the collar around her neck, which is attached to her shirt, and more of her becomes bare.

I can feel my pulse increasing as my eyes scan her form. Her skin is flawless! Textureless! Like white silk under water, to run your hands over it will meet no resistance, nothing but softness.

She is wearing a waist-cincher. I've never seen one on her before. This must be another new addition to her life. It's scarlet, eye-blinding red, almost neon, and it's tight, exaggerating her waist with almost wasp-like curves. Janice leaves that on and takes off her pants.

They slide off her skin like oil and pool on the floor like a tanker spill. Off her, they look like they could be rolled into a ball the size of a small orange. I wish I were the one unpeeling my lover from her second skin of latex.

Once again she isn't wearing panties, though I don't think one could in an outfit like that. Her hair hides the folds of her vulva, but it betrays her enjoyment otherwise. I can smell her clearly, that delicious scent that used to be perpetually on my fingers and tongue like some kind of free perfume, back when we were together. She still smells the same, and that's a comfort when so much else between us has warped and become unrecognizable.

I look at her boots. They are the only part of her clothing that I've seen before. Those boots, with the spiked heels and the pointed toe and the way they cause her foot to arch and her calf muscles to tighten in the same way they used to when I would make her come…I remember the boots. Janice must have known they'd cause flashbacks; that was the point in wearing them. Yeah, they're causing me to recall certain nights, flashbacks to taking them off her. I feel a flood between my legs and know my mind is not the only thing that has memories.

Janice leans forward and runs a hand along the boot and I'm nearly drooling with anticipation. She unzips one, steps out of it and casually tosses the boot behind her. She winks at me. I swallow hard and move in my seat, crossing my ankles.

The other boot ends up with the first. I notice her toenails are unpainted and that she isn't wearing the ankle bracelet I once gave her. No matter, it was only a gift.

I'm thinking of the past when I feel a touch on my right hand and the chains clank together. She's undoing me.

"Ayesha, take it off me." Janice turns around and I look at the black laces that criss-cross her waist and gently touch the white flesh in the spaces. It's like reaching out and touching Nirvana and she knows it. I hear her smiling as I untie the laces, slowly, like the unwrapping of a great and beautiful present.

As the laces get looser I see more and more of her nakedness. I resist the temptation to kiss her expanding flesh. Minutes pass and the corset gets looser and she becomes more and more bare, less clothed and constrained. The way our relationship is now, this is our sex.

Finally it's removed. There are red marks like whip lashes across her back from the pressure. I touch these hard ridges of skin and hear her gasp, her first sound of pleasure of the evening. I can't help myself, I smile and stand up, moving close to her naked skin with my clothed body. I kiss her shoulder and she turns to face me.

"Let's go to bed," I say, and walk unsteady across the floor, my legs shaking with nervousness. I sit on her bed's rumpled sheets and look expectantly at her. Janice has been unbound, unclothed, again she stands before me and just by viewing her do I get what I want—memories. Her eyes scan my face, looking for something, trying to read me, but there is nothing there. We've had our fun in the game of teasing and watching. It's all over now.

I want to remember this night tomorrow when she makes me breakfast and tells me to leave. I want to remember it next week when I'm sleeping alone wishing I could by lying beside her. And next month, when I see her at some bookstore and she pretends to not know me. I want to remember this night and how I undressed her, not just literally, but emotionally. I stripped her of her beliefs and challenged her on love's great shore and watched her walk away. I shouldn't remember these things, but I do, and always will.

You can't forget Janice once you've seen her naked.

DRESSING DANA
by R.F. Marazas

Just after six and I am on my way to my lover.

The closed sign hangs in the front door of the boutique. I picture him inside, waiting. I picture the hands with those long slender fingers. My thighs quiver.

Inside, the bell above the door gives off its quiet tinkle. The overhead fluorescents throw soft flattering lighting. I pause, looking down the endless racks of dresses, skirts, tops, undergarments. The room is cool and silent. Along the wall to the left, the dressing booths are empty except for one.

Guy doesn't look at me, but he knows. He's seen me come in. Those long fingers tremble. He waits at the one occupied booth for the door to open. It does. A gray-haired matron in a dress too youthful for her bulky body appears, her face flushed. She flashes an irritable scowl in my direction, which I ignore, slowly making my way toward the office in back, pausing to caress the silk of a blouse. I have interrupted her personal fitting by Guy Rocksson.

They all come here: the matrons, the restless marrieds, the teachers, even the young college students. They may go to the new mall or the more fashionable boutiques owned by impeccably dressed women, but they always return here. Guy does the fittings. If his hands brush against a breast or inner thigh or rounded bottom no one complains. If his fingers linger on warm bare flesh a beat too long no one is offended. Beth, giggling, whispered to me once that he almost made her come as he knelt in front of her brushing out the wrinkles in a dress she was trying on, his hand on her belly just above her mound. Beth loves to mock, but she more than anyone else is responsible for the growing legend.

She doesn't know. None of them knows. They feel safe with this harmless bachelor with the effeminate gestures, unthreatened by his apparent ignorance of what effect his hands have on them. They tremble and blush at the sensations, comfort themselves with the conviction that his concentration is on the clothes. They enjoy their secret thrills. I know what my friends think of me. Beth, Amanda, Val. They call me Miss Prim. I've heard them whisper that Guy and I would make the perfect pair, both dull. Let them.

In the small cramped office, I close the door and lean against it. My body feels ripe, breasts fuller, hips swollen. I remove my clothes, sweater, blouse, mid-calf skirt, pantyhose, bra and panties, low-heeled shoes. I stand there waiting, unsure of what to do with my hands, breath caught in my throat.

The door opens. Guy hardly glances at my nudity, the flush on my pale skin. His boyish face is serious, apprehensive. Light gleams off his bald head as he turns his attention to the antique wooden dressing closet. Next to it stands an antique mirror, full length, oval, its frame finished in polished, intricate scrollwork. My reflection is distorted because of some flaw in the glass. I stare at the full breasts with their pale colored nipples stiff with arousal, the wheat colored triangle between parted thighs. Guy is unaffected. There is no stirring, no bulge in his trousers.

"May I dress you?" he asks. So formal.

"Do you want to?"

"I've waited two weeks."

"Yes, you may." My breasts tingle.

Guy opens the closet and makes a pretense of choosing from his collection. As if he hadn't already made the choice.

I wait, standing erect, my legs rubbery. Inside the door, a thin leather riding crop hangs from a hook.

He sinks to his knees, his quickening breath a warm flow across my sex. My lips contract and then open, spreading in the warmth. First the stockings, sheer and silky. While I balance myself with a hand on his shoulder, he rolls each stocking slowly up my leg to the top of my thigh, his hands tracing patterns. Then the garters, with little blood-red rosettes adorning them. Again his hands caress every inch of covered flesh from thigh to ankle, smoothing. I feel moisture between my parted legs. Now the drawers, billowing silk with vertical slits back and front and a ribbed hem line. He draws them up, ties them at both sides.

He rises slowly, his face inches from my hidden sex. It's all I can do to restrain myself from pulling his face to me. Instead, I raise my arms high, lifting my breasts. I glance down at his growing erection. He slips the frilly petticoat down over my head, down my torso, and his thumbs flick across my hardened nipples, sending waves of sensation through me.

Next comes the lacy chemise, which he tugs gently over my aching breasts. It is snug, scraping my nipples until I feel they might burst. The dress is virginal white, and Guy takes his time with the buttons down the front, savoring the press of his fingers into my yielding flesh. He holds my fingers in his longer than he should, at last sliding on the gloves made of soft kidskin, a tiny pearl button at each wrist. For a moment, he stands back to admire his handiwork and I give him a stern, impatient look. He bites his lip in shame and bends to slip on the white shoes, fitting them to just above my ankles, buttoning them at the sides.

He holds the hat with the wide floppy brim and the band of bright blue ribbon around it and pauses again, looking at my short hair with longing. Perhaps I'll let it grow longer so he can pin it up as he wishes. My friends will wonder at this daring in the mousy Miss Prim. He places the hat, tilting it an inch, and steps back again.

"Lovely, so lovely."

We stand there transformed, the professor of Victorian Studies now a Victorian maid, the boutique owner and collector of Victoriana now her ardent suitor. He waits, his breath stopped. And I want him to wait, I want to prolong the agony for both of us.

"Bring me the riding crop." With the clothes my voice has changed. The plodding monotone that makes my students drowse is gone.

Guy hesitates, then turns to the closet. He carries the crop balanced on the tips of his fingers, his eyes fixed on it.

"You touched me again, took liberties with me."

"No!" But he blinks and lowers his head. I move closer to take the crop. His eyes are riveted on it. He is a statue, his penis bulging. I slide the crop tip up the length of him. He shudders.

"Look at yourself. You should be ashamed! Is this what happens when you dress the others?"

He nods.

"Answer me!"

"Never like this, with you. You're the only one..."

"Oh, you enjoy dressing them, don't you, you love to touch them. Don't you?"

"I can't help it, yes...but you, when you let me dress you this way..."

"You should be punished for your brazenness, shouldn't you?"

"Please!" He flings his arms around me, crushing the dress.

His erection presses against me through the dress and the petticoat and the drawers. Only when I dress this way is it so hard.

When I first came here—my friends daring me—afraid and tense yet stubbornly refusing to be cowed again, I thought he saw me as all men see me, that is, not at all. He dressed me, touched me, and was unmoved. And then I went to his office and saw the closet and took out a chemise...I know the ritual, the desire, the secret, as the others can never know it. It is mine now.

"Stand back!"

He obeys, trembling, eyes stealing glimpses of me. I tear at his belt, drag his zipper down. "Show me. Let me see your shame."

He struggles with his trousers and his penis bursts out before his shorts fall. The glans is shiny slick. The shaft towers above his navel, pressed hard against his stomach. The thought of him inside me almost weakens my resolve. But the ritual must continue. The sense of power is as exciting as the thought of him inside me. My voice is husky, firm with command. "Bend forward! Hands on the desk! Move your legs apart! Wider!" I grasp him with one gloved hand, the heat of him burning through the soft material. He groans, writhes in my grip. "Don't you dare lose control!"

His buttocks are tense, clenched. I grip him harder and bring the crop around in an arc. The crack is loud in the tiny room. He bolts forward, his penis thrusting into my gloved hand. Another stroke brings a cry from him. I plant my feet firmly, settling into a steady rhythm, gripping him tightly, my other arm a blur as the crop bites into him, counting the faint pink stripes as they appear on his pale flesh.

Finally his legs buckle; he sinks to his knees. I am trembling, the crop dangling from my hand. Guy turns and shuffles forward to embrace my legs, burying his face in the dress, in my sex. I feel his lips, his mouth, grinding. A shudder runs through me, a tiny explosion of sensation. The room is quiet except for our hoarse breathing.

He gets to his feet, his eyes glazed. I reach for him but he whispers, "Please, I can't hold back!"

I turn to the desk where he has just been, bend forward, place my hands where his hands were. I turn my face to the mirror. The distorted tableau shimmers and ripples on the glass. The Victorian maid, her dress rucked up above her waist, the frilly drawers stretched tight across her swelling buttocks. Her lover, grasping himself with one hand while the other parts the slit in the drawers. His penis slowly disappears into the opening. He thrusts. Their mouths are open now, their moans mingled, their bodies fused, his hands on her hips, her gloved hands stretching behind searching for his bruised buttocks.

The image swims in my blurred vision as his flood gushes into me and I come with enough force to shatter a hundred mirrors.

Guy slowly collapses away from me, his whisper echoing along my throbbing nerve ends, "Oh Dana, Dana, Dana...", and I'm standing over him looking down, my breasts heaving in the snug bodice. I begin to peel off the gloves.

"I have papers to correct."

"Yes."

He is on his feet again, taking the clothes from me lovingly, brushing, folding. His eyes do not register my nudity. He closes the closet doors. In the mirror, I am anonymous again in my everyday clothes. My body seems to shrink.

"There's an auction this weekend," he says, "one of the old houses. So many lovely things, ball gowns and lacy corsets..."

I smile at him. "I hope you'll bid on them. Tell me, do you think I'd look well in a ball gown?"

"Oh yes," he says, his eyes glazing. "Yes."

LUCY LAID BARE
by Stephen Albrow

I had grown to detest that nightdress. Every night for the past three months she had come to bed wearing the thing. It was a long, flowing, ankle-length gown that did nothing to accentuate the curves of her luscious body. The despicable nightie was her way of saying that she wasn't ready to give herself to me, yet.

Right from the start of our relationship, Lucy had made it clear to me that she wanted to take things slowly. As we were both fresh out of mistaken first marriages, I could understand why she didn't want to rush. But three months is a long time, and I was getting tired of going to bed in my tightest boxer shorts to try and hide my erections from her. I felt awkward snuggling up to her back each night, knowing that I'd bulked up big in the erogenous zone. Then I'd wake up each morning to the same thing all over again. My cock was definitely sending out a message to Lucy, but *still* she kept on wearing that nightdress.

Often I'd dream about setting it aflame. That's how much I hated that ghastly gown. But still I waited, and I waited, making plenty of attempts to get around the problem along the way. I booked us reservations in high-class hotel rooms, but the nightdress traveled along with Lucy. One hot summer night I suggested that we take off all our clothes and go swim naked in the river, but Lucy just laughed at the thought...then she put on the nightdress and jumped into bed.

Unsurprisingly, the amount of sexual tension inside me was fast becoming unbearable. Every night, I went to bed hoping, and every night my hopes would get dashed. I was desperate to see Lucy naked, but it got so that I thought that it was never going to happen, and that's precisely when Lucy waltzed out of the bathroom wrapped in just a towel.

I was already in bed that night, my erection shielded by a pair of boxers. It wasn't quite a total hard-on when she first came into the bedroom, but once I'd seen her wrapped in nothing but a towel, it quickly stiffened to its full length and height.

"It's warm tonight," Lucy said, then she sat down on the edge of the bed.

"I'm feeling pretty hot, myself," I confessed. I thought about making a grab for the towel. It was covering her torso from just above her breasts, right down past her pussy and then a little way down her thighs. Her hair was wet and her legs were glistening from her recent shower. Was she just waiting for her body to dry and then she'd get into the nightdress? Or had she finally decided to get naked with me? God, how I hoped that it would be the getting naked option! I stared lustily at Lucy's long, slender legs as she crossed them one on top of the other. She saw me watching, then I heard her giggle.

"What's so funny?" I asked.

"Nothing," said Lucy, then I followed her gaze and noticed that she was staring over at the back of the bathroom door. Hanging down from a hook on the door was the bane of my existence, the evil floor-length nightie. "Actually, I was laughing because I know how much you hate my nightie—and you'll be happy to know that I don't need it any longer."

Still giggling, Lucy threw off the blankets that were covering my body, then she stared down at me. Her hand reached out and with a fingertip she drew a line along the

length of my erection. "I really have kept you waiting, haven't
I?"

"Any longer and I might have burst," I replied, then I
reached out and grabbed for the towel.

"Not yet!" Lucy shouted, slapping away my hand and
moving off the bed.

Lucy switched out the lights and then opened the drapes,
so that her body was lit only by the moonlight. Then, as if
unveiling a work of art, she unhooked the towel and let it
tumble down to the floor. A gasp fell from my lips. This work
of art was a nude—a study in blonde and pink. I blinked a
few times as my eyes adjusted to the moonlight, then I
surveyed the glorious curves of her body. I worked my way
up from her dainty ankles, to her narrow calves, then
wallowed in her full-bodied, womanly thighs. My eyes took
in her pussy, her slender stomach, and then her firm, haughty
breasts ready to be fondled and kissed.

Lucy was naked. Lucy was naked in front of me. I had
waited so long and it was finally happening....

"Come here," I begged. As she approached, I kicked off
my boxer shorts. I wanted to be totally naked for her, just
like she was totally naked for me.

Naked! It's funny in some ways, because in the past I've
always loved to see a girlfriend dressed up in stockings or a
corset or—oh, baby!—like a nurse, but on this occasion, all I
cared about was Lucy's own flesh. I longed to feel her
nakedness close to mine, with not a stitch of clothing to keep
us apart. Most importantly, not that dreadful nightdress that
hung from the hook on the back of the bathroom door. I hoped
that it could see what was happening, that it could see that
its days were well and truly numbered.

"So, do you like what you see?" Lucy asked as she climbed
up on the bed and lay alongside me.

No words could have conveyed my feelings any better than

the way that I began to kiss her right then. I wrapped my arms around her body, then pressed my mouth to hers. Lucy grabbed me round the waist and rolled both of our bodies right over. It was the moment that I had been waiting for ever since we'd first met. Finally, I had the opportunity to fully explore Lucy's birthday suit. I stopped kissing her lips and buried my head between her neck and shoulders before heading towards Lucy's succulent breasts. I reached them in virtually no time at all, then took one of her nipples inside my mouth. Lucy groaned as swirled my tongue all around. I was beside myself, unsure how to proceed. I wanted to spend hours on her beautiful cleavage, but I wanted more.

Slowly, I began to kiss my way further down her body, lingering for quite a while over Lucy's smooth belly, before taking a trip right down her curvaceous left thigh, languidly continuing my journey right down to her feet. I sucked each of her toes until she yelped with laughter, so I quickly moved my attentions back up to her thighs, then I zoomed in on her pussy.

Lucy squealed as my lips pressed to her. She was already sopping wet, and her juices tasted just like heaven to me. I pressed my hands beneath her ass and lifted her right up off the bed, so that her pussy pressed even harder into my face.

When I couldn't wait any longer, I reached down and took a hold of my cock. Lucy was ready, and I was more than ready, and I quickly moved forward and mounted her body. Our lips touched, then they came apart, as I guided myself into her. She let out a groan, and her groan became a long, drawn-out sigh.

"Oh, yes," said Lucy, as I began to pump my hips back and forward. I could feel her pussy squeezing me tight. My gentle thrusts would open her up, then she'd quickly tighten around my cock again. Together, we made a perfect fit, and that gave me so much confidence. After three months together, I had known that Lucy and I were compatible in every way, except, perhaps, in the one department that had still remained untested. But as I slid so snugly in and out of her, I knew that the last hurdle had been successfully jumped. It was clear that Lucy and I were made for each other. It was doubly clear when she started to come.

My slow, measured thrusts had brought her right to the verge of a climax. I felt her hands slap hard against my ass, then she forced my cock to jam in deep. When I then shaped to withdraw, she continued to press me down, so that my full-length stayed trapped deep within her. A sequence of orgasmic contractions made her tense around me. I had to concentrate hard to stop myself from climaxing, too, as the pulsations in her pussy grew ever more extreme.

Then, all of a sudden, Lucy let go of me, once again allowing me to continue my thrusts. I slammed into her with every ounce of power that I had in my body. Our bare naked bodies could not have been any closer. Feeling totally swamped by my lust for Lucy's nakedness, I thrust forward hard for the final time, coming from the raw excitement that I felt on feeling Lucy's naked body beneath mine.

As I lay on top of Lucy, her lips twisting and turning on mine, I felt so close to the woman that I loved that I knew that nothing could ever come between us again. Certainly not that hideous nightdress that had prevented us from connecting for far too long. From that moment on, it would have to make do with hanging on the hook on the back of the bathroom door, as opposed to hanging on my lover's perfect body.

Emotionally and physically, everything was now out in the open. We had shown ourselves to each other in our naked states and we'd both liked what we'd seen. It had taken us three months to make it happen, but boy was it worth the wait.

TATTOO YOU
by Mark Williams

Tina had more tattoos on her than any woman I'd known previously. Mostly, they were small designs, delicate and sexy, *so* sexy: a tiny pink rose on her left instep; a crown of thorns wrapped completely around her right ankle; a miniature sunshine, with four gentle rays exuding from it, on her right hip, near the bone; a black-and-white yin-and-yang tattoo on her stunning ass; a small cross on her back, near her right shoulder blade; and my favorite, a sunflower on her left breast—a gold-and-brown masterpiece of nature.

Tina didn't look the type to sport so much ink. That's why I found her artwork so alluring. She was the epitome of business during the day, working as a successful international banker. A poster child of professionalism, she dressed in conservative suits, with skirts that almost always fell well below her knees paired with dark, usually opaque pantyhose and sensible shoes. Her hair was often pulled back in a bun, and she preferred conservative make-up. Cool, calm, and always subtly in charge, she had the elegance of a ballet dancer coupled with a true sense of authority.

Actually, she intimidated the hell out of me when I first bumped into her on the bus to work. We exchanged a glance or two, but nothing more. She reached her stop before I did, and as she alighted, she turned back to briefly look at me again. I smiled uneasily, guiltily. She looked haughty, almost arrogant as she turned away. I thought I'd never see her again.

Two mornings later, I was proven wrong. There she was, seated in a grey pinstriped pantsuit, reading the *Wall Street Journal*. Classically elegant. I made it a point to inch closer to her. Once again, she caught me staring at her, but this time she smiled back. "Hello again," she said with a voice that oozed honey.

I blushed. "Good morning."

"Actually, it's far too humid for my tastes."

I noticed she was actually a bit moist on the forehead. I was surprised that someone so crisp could sweat. I fished in my rear pants pocket for a hanky, then offered it to her. She dabbed herself briefly, then looked me over. "I'll launder it and return it to you later in the week."

"But what if we never see each other again?"

"You'll just have to call me, won't you?" She quickly produced a business card from her pocketbook. I couldn't believe it. I never figured I was her type. I gave her my card, as well.

Our first date was an elegant dinner followed by a classical music concert. Tina carried herself with total grace, and I behaved like a gentleman. When I dropped her at her door, I received a polite goodnight kiss. It was exactly what I expected. The second date was much more casual—a light dinner followed by a Robert DeNiro movie. But even in jeans and a silky white blouse, there was something reserved and gentile about this woman. Despite that, as we talked throughout the evening, I began to feel we were quite a match. Her second goodnight kiss was much warmer, but still without passion. I knew I'd have to wait awhile for her to warm to me completely. On our third date, I took her to the ballet. It was a Friday night, and she met me from work, so she was again an image of conservative glamour. After the performance, we went out for coffee.

Sipping her latte, she eyed me with surprising gentleness.

As she put her cup down, she said, "This is our third date, Michael—I guess this is the one where we decide."

"Decide what?" I played along naively.

"Whether or not we're going to fuck each other's brains out," she replied matter-of-factly. "Based on your performances to this point, I'd say you have an excellent chance of that happening. Now why don't you take me home."

I was hard before she finished her last sentence. In the cab on the way to her place, I was all over her like a hungry animal. She smiled bemusedly. "Easy, tiger, we're not there yet."

When we were at last inside her door, I could barely contain myself. "Tell me what you want me to do, Tina...please," I said almost breathlessly.

"Undress me very slowly, and we'll go from there." As she seated herself, I slipped off her shoes and realized her legs were bare. She'd obviously found the opportunity to cleverly remove her pantyhose sometime between the ballet and our cab ride, and with her long skirt covering most of her legs, I'd never noticed. On my knees in front of her, I discovered the rose tattoo, then the ankle bracelet design. I'd never seen either until now. "God, those are sexy," I said.

"Lick them," she told me. I was more than happy to. I ran my tongue along her instep, and the silkiness of her skin delighted me. Eventually, I moved to her other foot and licked her bracelet tattoo. I inhaled a mixture of her scents while I licked and gently nibbled, alternating feet and legs every few minutes. I could have done it for hours if she'd wanted me to.

"I need to get out of this dress now." She stood. As I unzipped her from behind, I saw the cross on her back. "How many more do you have?" I asked.

"You'll see," she told me.

I ran my tongue along her back and shoulder, outlining the crucifix on her back. She squirmed as though ticklish. I hesitated. "Don't stop, honey," she groaned. Her perfumed scent was stronger now, and her skin was warmer and sweeter. I was intoxicated, totally helpless.

When her dress fell to the ground and she stepped out of it, she was down to a bright red lace bra and matching panties. It was then I saw the sunshine on her right hip, peering above the top of her undies. I dropped to my knees again, this time tugging her panties just low enough to have full access to the next tattoo. Once again, I began to lick the image—and Tina—for all I was worth. My hard-on was throbbing, but my only focus was on tonguing the wonderful designs on this beautiful woman. As I pulled her undies down lower, her yin-yang tattoo caught my eye.

I began to kiss her asscheek, which was soft yet firm. A well-toned ass, to say the least. Again, I ran my tongue over the design, almost dizzy with delight at how I was getting to know Tina's body. I'd completely lost track of time, yet nothing mattered but making her happy. Tongue on tattoo, over and over. With each lick, she seemed to soften. The corporate Tina was all but gone...this was the tattooed Tina I hadn't imagined under those business suits.

"My bra next," she commanded, and after unhooking it, I saw the sunflower on her left breast. Small but striking. I gently pulled her down to her knees with me as I licked and sucked this last work of art. By now, her scent was one with me. Finally, I could take no more and gently bit her nipple. She moaned and began to shudder. "Oh God, yes," she cried, in the early throes of what would be a powerful orgasm. I gently nibbled on her again, and she continued to come, shaking and shivering as she forced herself against me as much as possible.

I realized as she was finishing her climax that the tattoos

were simply a road map to her pleasure zones. I apparently had followed the atlas perfectly to her specifications.

And they say men never ask for directions....

NAKED ON 47TH
by Lynne Jamneck

She didn't think I would come.

I may be a young punk with a guitar, but I'm punk enough to make good on a promise. She underestimated me—her and her *Queer As Folk* sensibilities. The burnished, executive elevator took its sweet time up to the 47th floor. Each time it made a pit-stop, people came and went. They'd look at me, of course, and I don't think it was because I'm famous. They didn't seem the type to have AlterSexed CD's in their collections. Not sure how many pierced chicks graced their lawyer offices, either. My T-shirt proclaimed *Fuck Off! I Have Enough Friends* in white on red.

Appalled, they were. But secretly they liked it—I know the type. I was hip to their facades.

Finally: 47.

Robin's office was down to the left. A corner job with a solid wood double-door that could've been the entrance to God's inner sanctum. The secretary gave me a suspicious look of disapproval. I must not have agreed with her Donna Karan outfit.

"And you are?" she deigned to ask me when it was obvious that I wasn't going to leave.

"Just press the little white button on the phone, and tell Robin that Lou's here to see her."

"You don't have an appointment. Sorry. Ms. McKenna is very busy." The pale thing smiled at me perfunctorily, then picked up her ringing phone. I walked up to her desk, and, with a nimble flick of my finger, disconnected the call.

"What the hell do you think you're doing?" she ice-queened me.

I smiled sweetly. "Nothing—yet. Now tell Ms. Mckenna she has a visitor, or I'll make a scene. I'll huff and puff and I'll blow the fucking house down. I can tell you're the sort who wouldn't like that. Now, push the button. There we go."

She conversed with someone on the other end of the line. Hopefully, the object of my affection, and not security. She replaced the receiver, and nodded stiffly in the direction of the two big doors.

"That wasn't so difficult, was it?" I patted her head gently as an afterthought. Had she possessed the ability to shoot poison from her eyes, I would've dissolved to a murky puddle on the spot, staining the stylishly beige carpeting.

Screw her. Hell—she *wished*.

I made sure to close the door behind me. Robin was on the phone. She had the receiver pinned between cheek and shoulder, one hand skimming through a stack of files, the other scrambled an expensive pen across an executive notepad. Her cheeks blushed a sexy pink as she offered me a look, before returning her flustered attention back to the caller. As she hung up the phone, the night before flashed in my head:

Dark and hammering, the club downtown. The two of us crammed into the tight bathroom cubicle. The drunk taste on her tongue and her insistent hand on my ass—

"Lou." She folded her arms, and gave me the once-over.

"Robin," I returned, cocked eyebrow for effect. We could have been a movie.

She spoke into the speakerphone: "Sheryl, hold my calls please. I do not want to be interrupted."

God, she was so professional. Quicksilver shiny. So not my type. What the hell was I doing here? Last night—*that's* what I was doing here. When Robin had been anything *but* professional.

"Your secretary doesn't care for me much," I confessed.

"Sheryl doesn't like anyone. That's what makes her such a good *assistant*."

She was teasing me. Trying to show me that I was being politically incorrect. In my opinion, if you sit behind a desk and answer a phone, you're a secretary. She could no doubt sense my view on the issue. I didn't care; my eyes were too busy trailing the inviting line of buttons on her crisp *(Chanel?)* shirt. Curt, sharp lines that accentuated the curve of her breasts underneath. My hands were just itching to unbutton the blouse. I wondered if she was wearing the pencil skirt. The one she told me about the night before, the one she said I could take off if I came to visit. She was such a cocktease. One might not think it just by looking at her, but I knew better. I'd experienced it first hand. *Lead you into a musty, cramped bathroom stall, work you into a frenzy. Stick her hand down the front of your pants and then had the balls to comply to the buzzing of her beeper.*

God bless you, Ms. McKenna.

"So, are you going to stand by the door all day?"

"I dare say, hopefully not."

She patted the edge of her desk, and I felt an involuntary spasm zip from my stomach, fanning like butterfly wings down to my groin. I had a sudden reflection of what Robin must look like in the throes of a vicious court battle. Without a doubt, she could impassion a jury to the point of moral injustice. She could probably veer between Queen Bitch and the Justice League at the drop of a hat.

Robin leaned back in the swivel chair as I slid onto the desk, my T-shirt screaming in her face. And lo, there was the pencil skirt, bouncing a dub of its own right back at me. She offered me the same cheeky tilt of her lips which had made me follow her into that bathroom in the first place. My hand reached for the top button of her shirt. I expected it to tremble with anticipation but, satisfactorily, I found myself steady as a rock.

"Hope you don't hold it against me," she said matter-of-factly. "Rushing out of there last night."

With the first button undone, I could glimpse the inviting swell of breast, cupped in white lace.

"You lawyers—lives dictated by the chime of your cell phones and the drone of your pagers."

"Rock stars —your sordid lives dictated only by the riff of your axe and the riff in your pants."

I offered her a surprised smile. Not so much for the last part of her statement (which, really, tended to be true), but more because this partner-in-a-prominent-lawfirm used words like axe as if she herself had been the cover queen of *Rolling Stone.*

With the second button popped, I simply had no choice in the matter. I allowed my hand to sneak underneath the cold, crispness. Her Übermodel-breasts fit into my hand like fresh, ripe peaches. I had to suppress the urge to just bend down and fasten my lips to them.

The shrill buzz of the phone made my hand apply an uncontrolled squeeze. Gooseflesh went racing down my neck as Robin's yet unseen nipple contracted to a tight pinch beneath the palm of my hand. She yanked the receiver to her ear, cheeks flushing again. I had the distinct feeling that I was being treated to a certain part of Counsel Mckenna few of her stiff-lipped colleagues even suspected existed.

"Didn't I tell you that I was not to be disturbed, Sheryl?" While she listened, I unbuttoned the rest of her shirt, and trailed a line down to the zipper of her skirt.

"Tell him to leave it with you. No, he can't." All the while, managing to keep her tone even. Robin alternated between looking at my hand, slowly pulling down the zip, and my eyes, which were already promising her a multitude of delights if she kept those doors closed.

"For God's sake, Sheryl—what do I pay you for? I'm in the middle of an extremely important meeting. If anyone comes through that door, you're fired."

Robin's words were becoming louder, harsher. I wasn't quite sure whether it was because:

a) she was really becoming agitated, or

b) because I'd bent down on both knees, kneeling between her legs so as to better roll down her sheer stockings. Even these were designer. I tossed them underneath the desk, along with her Prada shoes. Robin chucked the receiver down in its cradle.

The first sign of her professional façade cracking beneath the pressure of my tongue, traversing down her milky thigh. With my mouth in the hollow of her knee, I ordered her to take off her shirt. She complied without hesitation. I got the distinct feeling that Robin liked being given orders, seeing as she was the type to normally give them.

As I grabbed two silver-knuckled fistfuls of her skirt, Robin lifted her highly paid butt ever so slightly in the chair. There was a slick sound as the silk lining slid down against her naked skin. Underneath the Abe Lincoln desk it went with the other goodies.

"I object to that," Robin mused. Her voice had dropped at least two octaves since her discourse with Sheryl the waif— nay, wench.

"Object? Just like a lawyer."

"Here I am, naked except for my carefully chosen underwear. And you, with every stitch in place."

Carefully chosen underwear. She'd stood in front of her mirror, dressing herself in little slips of silk for me. Thinking of me. Hoping I would come.

Without a word, I slipped the cuss of a T-shirt over my head. I was in my paying-homage-to-the-sixties phase, and wasn't wearing a bra. In fact, I wasn't wearing any underwear, period. This would also be the first time I stood semi-naked in front of a high-rise window.

I was still contemplating whether it was window-washing day at Doyle, McKenna and Smith, when Robin hooked her fingers round one of my belt loops and pulled me onto the chair. More importantly—onto her. Her tongue in my mouth was hot and unsafe.

Not for the first time I realized that only an unlocked door separated our mid-afternoon tryst from public scrutiny. But what the hell did I care anyway? Voyeurism was but one of the lewd little secrets in my famous closet.

Robin moved her lips from mine to my shoulders, then started kissing the tribal tattoo which commenced its pointy trail in my neck, before curling itself down across my left breast and round to the small of my back.

"I've seen these before." She started unbuttoning my fly proficiently. "If I'm not mistaken." Her lips sucked softly, each of my nipples in turn. The butterflies in my groin had magically transformed themselves into fire-breathing dragons. "Isn't there a naughty little angel etched on the inside of your thigh?"

Ah, the *NME* photo shoot. It had shown most of my skin-etchings in all their glory.

I was particularly proud of that interview. Naked, bare— my skin and my Ovation. Subsequently, I'd shown off that angel in a couple of dark corners. I had no idea that dykes in the upper echelon of society would see them, too.

Once again, Ms. McKenna, you're full of surprises.

"I'd have pegged you more as a *Marie Claire* type of reader."

"Appearances can be so misleading." Then a surprised, contented smirk of a laugh escaped her mouth as she discovered my lack of underwear. I laced my hands round her back, unhooked her trusty Wonderbra, and threw it out the window. I had no idea it was open. Call me brainless, but I was concentrating on other things since the minute I walked in the door.

"You'll pay for that," Robin said, hitching me closer onto her lap. 'Those things are bloody expensive." She accentuated the last word by entering me, finally, mercifully.

I could feel the seams of my Diesels strain against her hand as it tried to get deeper.

Take the fuckers off! I wanted to shout, but the prospect of her hand moving from its current position didn't appeal to me at all. All I could do was kick my booted heels to the floor and hang on, watching the muscles of her stomach work, the fine line of hair running from her navel down into her slight underwear. Damn me for not taking them off earlier. As the weight of pressure built inside me, dancing round Robin's fingers like a troop of perverted bongo drummers, I realized that the walls of her office might look thick, but that wasn't necessarily the case. If we stayed at the heavy breathing currently resounding round the confines of the room, things would be dandy. But already, words like "Oh is that it?" "Harder?" "I dare you," and "Don't. Don't stop!" were spiraling between us in an atmosphere of skin and sweat. And then in a rip of soft fabric, Robin's panties were finally off, if unusable from then on in. She brought it on herself though. I wasn't thinking anymore at that point, only doing. Seemed I didn't know my own strength. She could send me the bill. All I cared about was that she was finally naked. The sight of her exposed crotch against the faded denim of my jeans managed to send me floundering over the edge. I grabbed onto the desk's thick edge with one hand, the other scrambling for the back of the chair as I grit my teeth in a convincing effort for silence.

"Next time, please remind me not to wear any undies," Robin teased into my ear. There was a wet sound as her naked back disengaged itself from the leather chair. I tried to stand up, but my knees buckled and I fell back, taking Robin down with me.

Ten minutes later, as I made my grand exit, I could still feel the heat in my back pocket from where Robin had stuffed her torn underwear. I smiled nonchalantly at Sheryl, who was busy talking on her phone. Couldn't help but notice that she smiled back awfully friendly. Couldn't help but notice the pink hue of her cheeks either, rushing madly down towards her neck as I gave her a wicked little wave of my fingers.

MULTIPLE NUDITY
by Sage Vivant

Moira stared mutely at Daniel, just long enough to make him chuckle with satisfaction. The sea breeze grew stronger as the little boat sped toward the patch of land a mile or so away. Finally, she found words.

"You *rented* an entire island?"

"Yes, I told you. We both need the escape. It's just for five days, but it'll do us good. Besides," he drew her close and some of her hair whipped his face, "I love you and want you all to myself."

Moira embraced him. She didn't know what special act she'd performed to deserve Daniel, but here he was, loving her. The more joy he brought her, the more fearful she sometimes became of losing him. She could count on one hand the number of times in her life she'd even received flowers from a man, and now here was Daniel renting an entire island for her!

The island, near Tahiti, sat nestled in a tropical mist that hovered at the tips of its lush trees. Thick, verdant foliage covered the ubiquitous hills. As the boat approached the island, Moira noticed several small huts built on stilts lining the shoreline.

"What are those? Are there other people here, too?" she asked, slightly disappointed at the prospect.

"There's a doctor, a chef, a maid, a maintenance man, and a masseuse on the island," the helmsman explained as he helped Moira and Daniel gather their belongings for disembarking. "I'll introduce you now but you need never see these people if you don't want to. They're at your service." They laughed with delight. Moira raised her eyebrows at Daniel as if to say *How about that?*

A small vehicle slightly larger than a golf cart awaited them. A tanned, well-built man who must have been the driver walked toward the three of them. As he approached, Moira was mesmerized by the contrast of his brilliant blue eyes with his jet-black hair. He had the smooth, sensual darkness of an islander but his height and blue eyes suggested some ethnic mix. He smiled, revealing perfectly white teeth.

"Welcome to Hedonis! My name is Hiro," he extended his hand for shaking. Moira was not surprised that it was warm and gripped hers firmly. "I am the maintenance person here. I drive you when you don't want to walk and I fix anything that may not function. I take care of everything that the others can't!" His smile was genuine but Moira could not place his accent. British with a splash of Spanish? It was disarmingly sexy, whatever it was.

The boat driver left them and Hiro introduced Moira and Daniel to the rest of the staff. Moira began to feel she was in some sort of Hollywood reality. The rest of the staff consisted of four astoundingly beautiful women: Pilar, the raven-haired, busty doctor (Moira silently prayed for Daniel's health); Shakti, the lithe, redheaded chef; Kareen, the tall blond maid; and Rayna, the shy but stunning masseuse. The introductions were courteous and brief. Moira and Daniel learned that assistance from any of these women or Hiro could be obtained by calling them directly from the phone in their hut.

Hedonis was only about three square miles and Hiro drove them to their hut in less than five minutes. Like those of the staff, Moira's and Daniel's hut sat on stilts affording it a view of the ocean. Although surrounded by trees, the house was not shaded; sun streamed into the numerous skylights disguised by what looked like a thatched roof.

Once inside, they discovered their "hut" was actually an 1800-square-foot bungalow with every modern convenience imaginable. The bedroom lay beyond the shallow foyer, with a wall of glass that exposed the sea. Hiro unloaded their bags, gave a swift tour of the house and slipped away to leave the lovebirds alone.

Moira threw herself happily on the king-sized bed and squealed with delight. "Daniel, look at this! A mirror over the bed! Isn't this fabulous?" Already, she could feel stirrings between her legs.

Daniel climbed onto the bed and began to kiss her neck. She felt her body instantly flush and unconsciously pushed her pelvis into his. Their mouths met tenderly at first, then more insistently. Moira wanted him but didn't want to explore her hunger right now. She gently pushed at his chest to separate them.

"You know what I'd like?" she asked. Daniel looked at her expectantly, even indulgently. "Ever since we got here, I've had this incredible urge to be naked in all this luscious greenery. Let's go outside and make love."

They sprinted outside. It was late afternoon and the sun melded with the mist, infusing the air with brilliant humidity. Each step they took added another layer of hot, moist air to their skins.

Daniel led Moira by the hand through plush, grassy paths lined with moss-covered rocks and thick, colorful leaves. Up a small hill, loomed the entrance to a cave. Despite its cavernous opening, the inside sat cloaked in darkness. They exchanged silent nods of agreement and ran up the incline.

If Daniel hadn't held her hand, requiring her to follow him, she might not have crossed the threshold to the ominous darkness. She knew they were alone on the island, save for the staff, but sensed some mysterious presence as they inched into the black cave.

"Daniel, shouldn't we have flashlights? Suppose there are animals in here?"

"Don't worry. Our eyes will adjust soon enough. I'm sure we're alone," he said, gently groping for her face. Finding it, he planted his mouth on hers.

As their tongues wrestled, they began fumbling with each other's clothes. Their minimal ensembles quickly unbuttoned, unfastened and slipped to the sandy cave floor.

The air in the cave was cool and surprisingly fresh. Daniel's hands squeezed her ass as he pulled her toward him. She grabbed at his pectorals. They continued kissing as Daniel nudged her to walk backwards. Moira assumed he wanted to press her against the wall of the cave, and so she stepped backwards, waiting to feel rock against her backside. Instead, two large, soft breasts pressed into her back. She yelped in response and turned to face her voluptuous attacker.

Enough light filled the cave for Moira to discern Pilar's stately physique. Moira stammered with embarrassment and no small amount of fear. What was Pilar doing here? And naked, at that!

Moira turned to Daniel for a good dose of masculine intervention but he merely stood, unfazed by Pilar's sudden and impertinent appearance.

"Would you like to lie down, Moira? There is a small bed right there," Pilar suggested in that authoritative tone so common to doctors. She gestured to Moira's left. Suddenly, Daniel's hand on her elbow guided her toward what seemed to be an elevated cot draped with a white velvet covering that glowed in the cave's darkness. Her eyes seared through the darkness at Daniel with inquisitive confusion. He stared back with a frustrating blankness; yet, she knew to trust him.

Silently, she lay down as instructed.

Daniel stood at her feet, calmly rubbing and stroking them. Without warning, Pilar's full mouth was on hers, her long, dark hair falling forward and brushing Moira's breasts. Moira instinctively moved to free herself but Pilar's hands moved to pin Moira's shoulders to the bed. Moira's cries of protest were muffled inside Pilar's mouth.

The soft strength of the woman disarmed Moira and she stopped struggling and relaxed into the kiss. She tensed, though, when a delicate finger began tracing the outside of her right nipple. Pilar applied renewed pressure to her shoulders, reminding Moira to stay put, but also emphasizing the existence of a new presence at the bed.

Moira opened her eyes. Although Pilar's dark head obscured her view, she noted that someone had lit candles around the cave. She still didn't know who was at her breast, but the hand felt like that of a woman. Her nipples responded to the circular teasing by growing and hardening, their silent way of asking for more.

Pilar separated her lips from Moira's. Moira then saw that Shakti stood by her right, but as Pilar had pulled away from Moira's mouth, Shakti had leaned down toward Moira's ready nipple and continued her tracing motions with her tongue. Pilar released her hold on Moira's shoulders, sensing her capitulation. She took Moira's left nipple in her mouth and imitated Shakti's oral teasing.

Moira looked down at both women, each with one of her tits at their mouths, and finally allowed herself to enjoy her own arousal. Heat flowed through her. The women's tongues continued to tantalize every part of her breasts but the centers; her need for more fired her insides. The nerve endings of her nipples clamored for direct stimulation. Why wouldn't they lick her nipples?

She looked at Daniel, still at the foot of the bed, holding

her ankles. His huge member stood at attention between her feet. He grinned at her with an odd mixture of lust and love, and it dawned on her finally that this had been his ultimate plan for their vacation all along!

She tried to shimmy her shoulders in an attempt to shake her nipples into the women's mouths. But the women ignored her movements. Their hands squeezed and caressed her tits while their tongues attended to everything but her nipples.

Daniel separated her legs suddenly but gently. Moira could smell her pussy and assumed everyone caught her scent. Instead of feeling shy, the knowledge that everybody was inhaling the aroma of her sweet juices turned her on. She was so wet she could almost feel her cream dripping.

Rayna appeared and climbed up on the bed, kneeling between Moira's legs. She radiated a powerful but gentle sensuality and smiled warmly at Moira. Her masseuse's hands followed the contours of Moira's legs from ankle to hipbone, slowly, deliberately caressing every inch. Moira could see the three women, but Daniel had disappeared.

Pilar and Shakti simultaneously lifted their mouths from Moira's engorged tits and straightened to face each other. Leaning toward each other while each holding one of Moira's tits with both hands, they French-kissed with an urgency that fascinated Moira. She watched them kiss, watched their hands knead and massage her impatient breasts and wondered if they'd ever just suck her desperate nipples.

Rayna's hands now worked her pelvis and pubic area with gentle, circular pressure. The cool cave air tickled Moira's wide-open sex. Did she want a woman between her legs? Rayna seemed kind and gentle, but she was female. Moira had only known big, manly fingers and pumping cocks. A woman couldn't satisfy her like a man could, she decided, but Rayna's soothing hands delivered fluid pulses of something that was at once relaxing and exciting.

Pilar touched one of her own nipples to Moira's and lightly rubbed. Shakti followed suit with her own tiny tits. The friction of the women's nipples against her own sent shock waves of pleasure through her body. Moira moaned quietly and matched her own movements to theirs to maximize the contact between their erect breast tips.

Almost instantly, Pilar pulled away, as if Moira's enjoyment was not to be indulged. Again, Shakti emulated Pilar and stood up straight.

"Why did you stop?" Moira asked, her heart pounding in her ears.

"You just take what we give you, don't you? Why don't you ask for what you want? Be strong! Tell us what you want!"

Moira stammered in confusion. Why was Pilar so stern with her? Why had she stopped being so attentive?

"I-I'd like you to keep doing what you were doing," she said shyly. She looked around for Daniel, hoping to get some support, but couldn't see him. "Daniel?"

"He stepped out. Stop being so dependent on him! Can't you ask for what you want?"

Moira's anger threatened to overtake her libido. "Of course, I can! I want you to suck my tits! Both of you! Put my tits in your mouths and suck!"

Pilar smiled, satisfied, and nodded to Shakti. Both women instantly began flicking their tongues against Moira's nipples and sucking ravenously. Her pussy gushed with a new round of arousal. The women lapped and sucked loudly at her. She wanted to know where Daniel was but the urgency of that desire began to dissipate under the sucking and licking at her breasts.

Rayna's fingers now played in Moira's pubic hair, dangerously close to her clit. "Wouldn't you like me to spread all this lovely juice over your pussylips, Moira? Can you imagine my fingers sliding over your hard, slippery clit?"

Oh, yes, Moira thought. A woman's fingers playing with her sounded heavenly. The women at her tits sucked hard in telepathic agreement.

"Yes," she replied meekly.

"Oh, Moira," Rayna said. "You'll have to be more convincing. I really need to know that you want me to finger your sweet little cunt." She continued to tickle Moira.

"Play with my pussy, Rayna," she commanded, excited by her own words. "Slide your fingers inside me and fuck me."

Pilar groaned at Moira's words, the sound vibrating through Moira's nipple.

Rayna's slender fingers gently but firmly began to burrow into Moira's succulent sex. She massaged her clit with the tip of one finger.

"That's better, Moira. Now, I know what to do for you," she said, frigging Moira's clit with quicker strokes. "You like to be finger-fucked?" She slipped her slinky middle finger into Moira.

"Yes. And use more fingers." Moira could hardly believe her own words.

Rayna slid two, then three fingers into Moira and pumped several times. Moira moaned and began thrusting herself into Rayna's hand to feel the digits inside her more deeply.

The women stopped sucking and moved away from the table in unison. Hiro and Daniel appeared at her right, both of them naked, sporting raging hard-ons. Rayna now fucked her with four fingers, in and out, in and out.

Hiro's cock was enormous and beautifully shaped. Long, thick and hard like a marble column, Moira thought, aching to stuff it into her. He ran his eyes over her body, lingering over Rayna's rapid finger-fucking.

"Turn to me, Moira," Hiro commanded.

Moira understood that she should turn on her side but didn't want to interrupt Rayna's attentions to her hungry cunt. Pilar stepped to her left side and slipped both hands under Moira's left shoulder. She nudged Moira to roll to her right side and Moira obeyed. Rayna pulled her hand away.

Her new position put Hiro's cock inches away from her face. Daniel stood next to him.

"It's a beautiful cock, Moira. I know you'd like to suck it," Daniel said, stroking her hair affectionately. "I don't mind if you do."

Her mouth consumed Hiro's cock without hesitation. He was as hard and hot as she imagined. Pilar stood at Hiro's right and played with Moira's tits as Moira gave Hiro a wet, messy blowjob.

Rayna sat on the bed with legs spread. She lifted Moira's top leg and moved herself in closer, until their pussies pressed together in juicy softness. Moira ceased sucking Hiro's cock for a moment to absorb the full sensation of Rayna's dripping pussy rubbing furiously against her own.

"Do you like this, Moira? Do you like feeling your clit licking mine?"

"Oh, yes, Rayna!" Moira called out, lost in heady ecstasy before continuing to suck Hiro's delicious cock while Pilar squeezed and stroked Moira's tits.

Kareen appeared and began sucking Rayna's full breasts. Daniel slipped behind Kareen and Moira saw that he was fucking the cleavage of her asscheeks.

The candlelight gave all of them an eerie, preternatural quality. With their eyes closed in sensual surrender, they appeared to be floating in hedonistic oblivion.

Moira knew her orgasm was imminent. She pictured the orgy in her mind, as if she were above it looking down. All those bodies and tongues, all that pleasure. She was so hot with lust, she could barely contain it. Daniel had Kareen's big tits in his hands now, too, and bounced them up and down from his position behind her.

Moira abandoned restraint and let her herself feel her gripping orgasm ignite somewhere deep in her pussy. It spread like a gasoline fire through her cunt then up and outward, convulsing every muscle in its wake. Never releasing Hiro's cock from her mouth, she came repeatedly, in succession, each spasm stronger than the next. She rode the waves of pleasure without conscious thought, revelling only in the primal pleasure of it all.

Moira had a vague recollection of being carried back to their hut. It all seemed like a wet dream to her now. As she lay spent and exhausted in their bed at the hut, Daniel explained how each day on the island would present new experiences in female love for her. She was to rest well to be ready to receive the staff's teaching. Moira grinned as she drifted off to sleep, eager to be a good student.

BARE NECESSITIES
by Ayre Riley

1) Oil
2) Towel
3) Beach
4) Charlie

That's it. For a hot summertime afternoon, those are the barest necessities that I require. Once I possess the ingredients, I can easily picture the scene in my head: me and Charlie out at Zuma Beach. The warm white-gold sand heating our crimson terry-cloth towel from beneath, the midday sun heating our bodies from above. And Charlie, my handsome dark-haired Charlie, spreading oceans of glistening suntan oil on me until my skin positively gleams. Charlie sliding his big, strong hands under my fuchsia bikini top to stroke my naked breasts. Charlie bending down to kiss the tender skin at the nape of my neck, then moving up to whisper, "I'm going to fuck you when we get home. Oh, baby, I'm going to fuck you so hard—"

And me sighing and leaning back on him, feeling his hard-on through his cobalt-blue surf shorts and sighing, "Yes, Charlie, yes."

Because that's all I need. Me and Charlie in a hot, public encounter, oblivious to the rest of the sunbathers around us, oblivious to anything except our naked arousal for one another.

In fact, for an even more stripped-down encounter, I'll amend my original lustful laundry list. Forget the other sunbathers. Forget the towel. Forget Zuma and the mid-day sun. For a raucous good time, all I need is:

1) Oil
2) Charlie

That's it. Me and Charlie in the center of our living room. My bathing suit discarded in a rippling pool of hot pink fabric. Charlie stripped out of his board shorts, his hands gleaming with oil as he spreads the tropical-scented lotion all over my body, making me shine as if coated with liquid gold. The scent surrounds me and draws me in. Charlie takes me from behind, pushing me onto my hands and knees, so that I immediately arch my back and ready myself for him. Doggy-style is my favorite way of fucking—or, really, of getting fucked. I like how strong Charlie feels behind me, how in control. I like when he grabs my long strawberry-blonde hair and holds me steady.

I like it all.

And now that I think of it, even that previous sexy list seems a bit wordy. A bit too cumbersome. For a good time, all I need is one thing. It's true. To make my heart beat faster, to make my body melt, all I need is:

1) Charlie

He's the one item I can never exclude. Charlie and me in our kitchen, fucking against the cool marble countertop, both of us naked, both of us primed from watching each other strip. Me and Charlie, all alone together. He takes me with a force that I have come to trust, that I have come to expect, to rely on, really. He pounds me hard, so that I can feel our connection in every part of my being. But even as he's thrusting into me with ever-increasing force, his hands work gently, cupping my breasts from behind, moving down my flat belly to part my pussylips and rub my clit in soft, slow circles, then heading back up again and stroking my ribs so that I tremble all over, on the very brink of losing control.

Charlie bites into my shoulder as he fucks me. He thrusts and stays sealed in firmly. He pulls back, and I am empty without him. Yearning, craving, borderline desperate. And when he strokes me inside again, strokes faster and faster until we both reach it, I know this to be the truth:

Charlie is my bare necessity. All I ever need.

NAKED? NEVER.
by Alison Tyler

I'm not a fighter, but I am never without my protection.

I'm not a warrior, but I always wear armor. As strong as iron. As tough as steel. I can't imagine leaving my apartment without it. I'd feel exposed. People would see me, *really* see me, and I couldn't handle that. As long as I am suited up, I feel powerful and in control. Without my gear, I would be naked, and that's an impossibility for me. For years my personal motto has been simply this:

Naked? Never.

My first piece of armor was a battered leather jacket purchased for sixty dollars at a Soho thrift store. Huge, black, and ugly, the thing had an attitude all its own. The sleeves hung well past my fingertips, and the body of the coat fell practically to my knees. From the moment I first put my hands through the sleeves, I knew its power. My stride lengthened. My dark brown eyes took on a sharper glow. My posture was straighter. When I wore that jacket, I felt strong. Immoveable. It was my cloak of invisibility. I'd slip it on and disappear into its welcoming depths. I can still close my eyes and conjure up the smell of the old leather, remember the softness of the interior, cave-like and warm. That special coat kept me safe for years, and even after its function faded, I stored it in the back of my closet, where I could stroke the surface for strength whenever I needed an extra charge.

In college, I discovered that I didn't have to disappear in order for my protective shield to be working. "All black" served the purpose just fine—even form-fitting, sexy black would work for me. In a sleek dress and killer high-heeled boots, I was unstoppable. In a velvet stretch-top covered with skulls, I exuded power. With my black hair, dark eyes, and pale skin, I could be goth without trying, dark without death. Nobody ever called me on my color choice. No one ever seemed to notice where my power came from. I reveled in my ability to get away with my secret—although I might appear finely waif-like and deeply feminine, I was never without armor.

It took several years of dating before I was forced to explain my style to a lover. All New Yorkers own closets filled with black. I'd simply turned mine into a sense of self-preservation. In my suit of armor, I am steel-coated. With dark ruby lipstick and an ice-cold stare, I am all-powerful. And while Jonah admired my expensive collection of clothes, he wanted to go beyond them. He wanted to find out about the woman beneath.

He tried subtle ways at first, attempting to undress me for sex. But I was on to him, and I took the lead. I undressed myself, down to the basics, and then I went on my knees and undid his fly and sucked him down. He forgot his intentions, swallowed up by his lust. He allowed me to keep on my satin tap panties and demi bra, reveling in the sensation of my mouth on his cock.

Only afterwards, collapsed on the sofa, he remembered how the evening had started.

"I wanted to strip you," he said, confused at the change of plans, but too sex-drunk to figure out how I'd taken over.

"I got to you first."

"But you never let me see you naked. You've got a killer body. Why hide it?"

I touched myself through the sheer undies. "I'm not hiding anything."

"You are," he insisted. "You dress up for me. You wear any sort of costume I request. But you won't let me see you bare," Jonah said. "So how about naked?"

"Naked? Never." The words slipped out before I could stop myself.

"Never?"

"Okay, right," I conceded. "In the shower. In the tub. Occasionally, in a private sauna. But no other time."

"Not even alone? When you're in your apartment all by yourself? What about then?"

How to explain? I couldn't. I didn't have the words. All I knew was that naked was not safe. Jonah waited, quiet, patient. I gave him a quick headshake, feeling my curls fall free around my flushed cheeks. I let my eyes glance downward to see if I really did still have my clothes on, and then I sighed with relief. Why? Because naked equals exposed. And I'm never exposed.

"Naked?" he repeated.

"Never."

"Never?"

I like my armor. After six years, I'm used to it. I'm protected.

"Even with sex?"

Definitely with sex. *Of course,* with sex. Different armor is called for during romantic interludes, but armor, nonetheless. Lingerie armor. Black lace armor. The sort of sexy nothings that men—at least, the men I've been with up to Jonah— have never understood counted for anything at all. But for me, they're as serious as battlefield armor. Even a G-string offers protection. I've never been entirely nude with a man. No previous lover ever thought to complain.

"Take them off."

I looked at the camisole and tap panties. They were sheer black, edged in lace. To me, they were made of steel reinforcements.

"No," I said, "No. Never...."

"Never." Jonah repeated, and I could see that he was trying to recall our past encounters. The merrywidow. The corset with stockings. The La Perla. The velvet-trimmed nightie. "Never," he repeated softly. "Okay, baby. That's gotta change."

My armor has protected me since I realized that I had a body. Since I decided to protect that body.

"Slowly," he said, but his tone was emphatic.

"Slowly," I repeated, looking into his bottle-green eyes. "So slowly." Thinking to myself: *Naked.*

Never?

We started with a game. He'd take off one piece of clothing. Then I would. His jeans. My black jersey dress. His T-shirt. My stockings. He didn't push me. He fucked me while I still had on my lacy crotchless panties and iridescent noire push-up bra. He fucked me against the wall while he whispered to me, "I'm going to take off all your clothes. I'm going to strip you down and look at you, really look at you." I shuddered all over, and then I came. Harder than hard. Harder than ever.

The next time, we went a step farther. "You undress me," he said. "You do all the work." I was on him immediately, and I liked it. I unbuttoned his top, undid his fly with my teeth. I spread the clothes around him on the bed and feasted on him. I got to stay dressed, and that made me feel invincible. The only thing I lost was my lipstick, spread around the base of his cock and up and down the shaft. When we were finished, I was mussed, but still protected. He was entirely naked, his body decorated with the blood-red stains of my lipstick kisses.

The night after, we got closer to the truth. After an evening spent at a dance club in the city, he stripped me. I felt my heart pounding. Heard the blood rushing in my ears. But he took pity once again. He got me down to my thong and bra set, then flipped me over and fucked me doggy-style, plucking the floss of the thong out of the way in order to gain entrance.

So maybe he did understand, I thought. Maybe he realized that fucking with clothes on was okay. Or maybe he was willing to give me this little flaw, this little mental glitch. Could it be that he'd leave it to the teasing? Telling me he would have me bare, but letting me slip away with something to wear for protection?

But no...

The next night, he requested a strip-tease. "It will be fun," he assured me. "Sexy and sweet." I knew I could have layers, and this eased my mind. I thought he would stop me before I got to the base. I thought he understood the fear that coursed through me. The music was cliche—silly even. But erotic almost in spite of itself. A standard; a classic: "You can leave your hat on."

"You can," Jonah said.

"Excuse me?"

"Leave your hat on."

"I'm not wearing a hat," I said, stating the obvious.

"You can *put* a hat on," he suggested, eyebrows raised.

I looked at his collection of vintage ball caps and then shook my head.

"Go on," he said. "Choose your armor."

"They don't offer much protection."

"You won't need any more. Trust me."

We stared at each other in silent battle. Then I shrugged and moved over to the wall. This was Jonah's game. I had to trust him or it wouldn't be worth playing at all. After a moment's consideration, I plucked a blue one from the rack and slid my ponytail through the back. "Now," he said, starting the music up again. With each piece of clothes, he said, "Tell why."

"Why?"

"Why you need any sort of armor in the first place."

"The looks," I explained as I peeled off my top.

"Looks?"

"From men."

"But it's me looking."

"I know."

"So what's the problem?"

I shrugged. I didn't really have a clue. All I knew was that naked was scary. Even with the little tender underthings, I could protect myself. But tonight was the night. Jonah wanted a complete reveal. As the music continued, I peeled off each item.

"Did someone every say something nasty to you?"

"Nasty?"

"Mean—"

I shook my head. That wasn't it. This wasn't about being judged. I simply have always reveled in the safety of being undercover.

"But what about the boldness of showing yourself off? Can't you see the power in that?"

I moved my hips to the music, and I thought about what he was saying. I was down to my black velvet bra and panties—and that ball cap. I saw Jonah watching me, and then I saw past him, saw my reflection in the mirror. Cocking my head at myself, I flipped the straps down my arms, showing Jonah my breasts.

It's not that I've never had a man look at my breasts before, or touch them, or play with them, but I've always had something on—a bra to kiss through, a sheer camisole, a bikini top. At twenty-two, that shouldn't be entirely shocking. But Jonah seemed to think so. He sucked in his breath as I pulled off my bra, and I suddenly understood what he meant. I did feel power. As powerful as when fully clothed.

"Please," Jonah said, reaching out for the waistband of my panties. "Please, baby—"

I grinned at him. This was a new feeling, this raw heat running through me. While gazing into his eyes, I slowly pulled my panties down my thighs and then let them drop to the floor. I was undressed, exposed, and radiant with desire. Jonah motioned for me to come to the bed. I took my time, still moving to the music. I knew that fucking this time would be different. I knew that fucking from now on would be different—that dressing would be different—that *everything* would be different.

Jonah gripped me around the waist and pulled me so that I was astride his naked body. I could look down at his handsome face, or look straight ahead at the reflection of my naked body. Both images were equally sexy. I slid my hips upward and then rocked down on Jonah's cock. He tilted his head back and groaned. I worked him harder, pumping my thighs up and down, riding him in a driven rhythm, back and forth. My clit gained contact with his flat stomach whenever I rocked my hips forward, and I could tell that this was going to make me come.

This and the power of being naked.

Nobody ever told me about that. Nobody ever explained that while you can gain protection by being draped from head to toe, naked can be even more extreme.

I pushed myself up on Jonah's long, lean body, then slid back down. I arched my back and pushed my breasts out to him, and felt his hands come up to cup them. I shivered at the sensation of his fingertips on my naked breasts—naked, entirely naked—and then I sighed as he let one hand slip down lower, finding my clit, touching me there without any barrier.

I sucked in my breath and slid up and down again, not shutting my eyes, not closing him out.

I could see the pile of my black clothing on his bedroom chair, and I thought how strange that puddle of blackness looked. What would I wear to get home? Not all that. Surely, not. What would I wear from now on?

Jonah tapped at my clit, and I locked eyes with him, and said, "I'm gonna—"

"I know."

"I'm gonna come—"

"You can leave your hat on," crooned Tom Jones, and I pulled that baseball cap off and tossed it to the floor.

My armor was inside. That's what I learned. I didn't need any battered jacket, any all-black wardrobe, any filmy nightie. I could be all-powerful wearing nothing at all.

Not even a hat.

EPIDERMIS EROTIQUE
by Jamie Joy Gatto

your skin,
smooth and fine, and nearly hairless
begs me to stroke it
and then I have to smell it
and of course, I must taste it
and when you are asleep
I lick it with my eyes
chin resting on your shoulder

I examine your broad, sinuous back
watch it dance, following the dip
into the valley of your waist
even lines, sure and fluid
as if belonging to a well-worn road
refined and easy to travel
with my palms, fingertips, moist lips

hips jut outward into girlish shape
but lie, because they meet
buttocks too firm to belong to a woman
round mounds of muscle flicker
with strength, and ripen under my gaze
an imagined bite into that peach of an ass
makes my mouth water,
I bite my lower lip and I sigh

I murmur too loudly, but still you don't awaken
and I am too shy to disturb your dreamscape
with my selfish, tactile desires
besides, my worship of your flesh
demands you lie still

and in waking life you never seem to stop,
no, never immobile, always going, running, dancing, diving
only here, in sleep, can I capture you
and hold you, savor you, feed my need to feel you

only now can I take the time
to touch your perfection
but I do it one breath away,
hands firmly at my side,
I touch you everywhere, yes
but I do so
only with my eyes

The Authors Unveiled

Stephen Albrow ("Lucy Laid Bare") was born and raised in the sunny seaside town of Lowestoft, England. Walking through its mean streets, he developed an eye, ear and nose for all things sexual and perverse. The things he saw and heard and smelled, he has since used as fodder for a whole host of filthy stories. They can be found in various notorious publications, such as *Swank Confidential*, *Penthouse Variations*, *Knave* and *Fiesta Digest*.

Eden Baltulis ("Stripping Janice") is a full-time student, freelance photographer and nocturnal writer. In her spare time she rides horses, collects obscure minerals, makes a wicked pasta salad, and sends postcards from places she's never been, to people she has never met. Any leftover time is devoted to either thinking about sex or having it. She is infamous for morally questionable poetry readings in numerous pubs and coffee shops across Canada and enjoys her reputation, which precedes her like a hurricane. She has been known to talk to strangers. She currently resides in a small town with a large sky.

Tenille Brown ("The Art of Exposure") resides in South Carolina with her husband and two children. Her work is featured in *Best Women's Erotica 2004* and *Swing! Third Party Sex*. Her first novel, *What It Looks Like From The Outside,* will be released in 2004, and she is currently compiling a collection of her erotic fiction, tentatively titled, *Skin*.

Tulsa Brown ("Radiance") is a Canadian novelist who recently crept over genre lines and is having a sinfully good time in erotica. Her work will appear in several anthologies, magazines and e-zines this year, including *Best Women's Erotica* and Black Lace's *Wicked Words*. Tulsa's mom believes she's writing something scholarly. Shh.

Rachel Kramer Bussel ("Touch") lives in New York City where she writes primarily about sex, smut, books, music and pop culture. She is the reviser of *The Lesbian Sex Book*, co-editor of *Up All Night: Adventures in Lesbian Sex*, co-author of *The Erotic Writer's Market Guide* and editor of the forthcoming *Glamour Girls: Femme/Femme Erotica*. She has written for publications including *AVN*, *Bust*, Cleansheets.com, *Curve*, *Diva*, *Playgirl*, *The San Francisco Chronicle* and *The Village Voice*, and her work can be found in over 20 erotic anthologies including *Best American Erotica 2004*, *Best Lesbian Erotica 2001* and *2004*, *Best Women's Erotica 2003* and *2004*, *Down and Dirty*, *Juicy Erotica*, *Naughty Stories from A to Z* 3 and 4, and others. Visit her at www.rachelkramerbussel.com

Work by **M. Christian** ("Jess Undressed") can be seen in *Best American Erotica*, *Best Gay Erotica*, *Best Lesbian Erotica*, *Best Transgendered Erotica*, *Best Bondage Erotica*, *Best Fetish Erotica*, *Friction*, and over 150 other anthologies, magazines and websites. He's the editor of over 12 anthologies, including *Best S/M Erotica*, *Love Under Foot* (with Greg Wharton), *Bad Boys* (with Paul Willis), *The Burning Pen*, *Guilty Pleasures*, and many others. He's the author of four collections, the Lambda-nominated *Dirty Words* (gay erotica), *Speaking Parts* (lesbian erotica), *Filthy* (more gay erotica), and *The Bachelor Machine* (science fiction erotica). For more information, check out www.mchristian.com.

Dante Davidson ("Naked New Year") is the pseudonym of a professor who teaches in Santa Barbara, California. His short stories have appeared in *Bondage*, the *Naughty Stories*

from A to Z series, *Sweet Life I* and *II,* and *Best Bondage Erotica* (Cleis). With Alison Tyler, he is the co-author of the best-selling collection of short fiction *Bondage on a Budget* and *Secrets for Great Sex After Fifty* (which he wrote at age 28). He dedicates this story to AM.

Steven Fire ("Nude Dreams or Naked Reality?") has tried being a newspaper reporter, minister, and teacher. His writing versatility ranges from horror, science fiction, and erotica. Some of his short stories have appeared in Justus Roux's literary anthology, *Erotic Tales,* and on 31eyes.com. Look for his novel, *Clone Hunter,* to hit stores in early 2004. Currently, Steven lives in Tulsa, still waiting to make a million dollars from his writing ability.

Jamie Joy Gatto ("epidermis erotique") is a widely published New Orleans native author/editor and activist best known for her erotica and sex-related non-fiction. She teaches adult sexuality classes and workshops, runs an international bisexual newsgroup and Web resource called A Bi-Friendly Place, manages an erotica author Web ring, and regularly performs spoken word to adult audiences. Jamie Joy is founder and editor-in-chief of the literary Web magazines www.MindCaviar.com, www.OpheliasMuse.com. She's authored *Sex Noir* (Circlet 2002) available in hardback, and has edited with M. Christian, *Villains & Vixens.* Gatto's collections *Unveiling Venus, Strictly Bi, Suddenly Sexy* and *Erotic Intelligence* are available at Renaissance eBooks (www.renebooks.com). Visit her at www.JamieJoyGatto.com.

As of writing these self-revelatory lines, **Maxim Jakubowski** ("Utterly Nude") is on a Caribbean island, most often in a state of undress, surrounded by beautiful women in a similar state of non-attire. Blame it on sun, sand and food, but this provokes little lust in his heart. However, in civilian life, he lives in London and rides the tides of sex, editing the best-selling Mammoth Book of Erotica anthology series, crime novels full of lust and yearning (latest is '*Kiss me Sadly*'), owning a mystery bookshop, organizing film and literary festivals and authoring columns for the Guardian and Amazon.co.uk., whenever his mind is not occupied by matters carnal. His newest novel is *Confessions Of A Romantic Pornographer*.

Lynne Jamneck ("Naked on 47th") has written for publications including *Best Lesbian Erotica 2003, On Our Backs, City Slab Magazine*. Photography has appeared in *Cure Magazine, DIVA, The International Journal of Erotica* and *Jade Magazine's Special Reserve Collection Book*. Upcoming fiction will feature in *Naughty Stories From A to Z Vol. 4* (Pretty Things Press), H.P Lovecraft's Magazine Of Horror, and the anthologies *Darkways of The Wizard* (Cyber-Pulp), and *Raging Horrormones* (Lethe Press). Ms. Jamneck is the creator and *Editor of Simulacrum: The Magazine of Speculative Transformation* (http://www.specficworld.com/simulacrum.html).

Kate Laurie ("Her Birthday Suit") has been writing short stories since she was a teenager, although this is her first published story. She first became interested in writing erotica when she wrote and read a story for a friend's bachelorette party. Since then her stories have become a staple at any of her friends' get togethers. She lives on the northern California coast with her husband and cat who patiently put up with being locked out of her office while she writes. Kate spends most of her free time traveling and camping, although her favorite activity is reenacting her erotic stories with her husband, James.

August MacGregor ("The Story Her Body Told") is the pseudonym of a writer and graphic designer who has recently jumped from the corporate ship into the turbulent and fascinating waters of freelance work. But he is learning to swim and, through his love of literature, visual concepts, and sensuality, has found an outlet in writing erotica. Currently, he is working on an erotic and historical novel. He lives in Maryland with his wife and two daughters.

R.F. Marazas ("Dressing Dana") is an English major who worked too many years in a profession having nothing to do with writing. His few and far between stories have placed in a few contests and been published in now defunct little magazines. Lately he has been published on the Internet in Writer Online, Sun Oasis, and Literoticaffeine. Retirement has given him time to dredge up all those stories he mulled over during the rat race years.

Jesse Nelson ("Stripped Down") lives with his girlfriend in Santa Monica where he spends too much time surfing and not enough time working. His short stories have appeared in *Sweet Life II* (Cleis) and *Naughty Fairy Tales from A to Z* (Plume). He dedicates this story to Hailey.

Alex M. Quinlan ("Bare to the Waist") lives on the East Coast of the United States, with children, spice, and pets of both the four- and the two-legged variety. Except when they're playing one of the myriad games that live in the bookshelf, they all spend too much time on the Internet, but not much at all on the World Wide Web. Unless, of course, they're attending a science fiction convention, anywhere from D.C. to Boston. More of Alex's writings from life, real and imagined, logical and virtual, can be found in *Unlimited Desires: an International Anthology of Bisexual Erotica*, on the website Clean Sheets (www.cleansheets.com), in Prometheus (www.tes.org), and in Consent (www.consentmag.com).

Ayre Riley ("Bare Necessities") has written for *Down & Dirty* (PTP), *slave* (Venus), and www.goodvibrations.com. She would like people to know that her name is pronounced like "Air" not like "Ayree."

After a career as a teacher, mother, and writer of a successful series of children's books, **Cate Robertson** ("Stroking") has recently turned her attention to literary erotica. In 2003, she has had stories published in such prestigious online venues such as Clean Sheets and Scarlet Letters. "Stroking" reflects her love of the sport of rowing. Cate lives in Canada with her husband of more than 25 years.

San Francisco writer **Thomas S. Roche** ("Sleeping Naked") is the author of more than 200 erotic stories, many of which are showcased on his website, www.skidroche.com. His ten books include *His, Hers, Dark Matter*, and three volumes of the *Noirotica* series of erotic crime-noir anthologies. Other recent projects of his include Noirotica.net, a weblog at http://thomasroche.livejournal.com, and a series of visual-art projects based on the Noirotica esthetic. His work appears frequently on Goodvibes.com.

Lacey Savage ("Barely Connecting") began her love affair with erotica at an early age. After reading every copy of *Playboy* she could get her hands on (all for the articles, of course), she later discovered the joy of sex in novels and anthologies. She initially majored in Marketing, then went back to school to major in English Literature. After earning her degrees, she decided to turn her efforts to her true passion: writing. A hopeless romantic, Lacey loves writing about the intimate, sensual side of relationships. She currently resides in Ottawa, Canada, with her loving husband and their mischievous cat.

Savannah Stephens Smith ("Naked Ambition") is a pseudonym designed to conceal the identity of a mild-mannered office worker on Canada's west coast who writes smut when no one is looking—and sometimes when they are. True to her passion, she enjoys books and words, paper and pens. Her fiction has been featured at the Erotica Readers and Writers Association and other online destinations. She has a weakness for glimpses of the moon, the blues, and Gibson's Finest whiskey. She used to smoke cigarettes, and now settles for just smoldering a little.

Wiley Smith ("What Do You Say to a Naked Lady?) lives in Marin County and travels the Point Reyes/Petaluma Road with great frequency. He has also written for www.goodvibrations.com.

Alison Tyler ("Naked? Never.") has written for anthologies including *Sweet Life 1 & 2*, *Wicked Words 4, 5, 6, & 8*, *Erotic Travel Tales 1 & 2*, *Best Women's Erotica 2002 & 2003*, *Guilty Pleasures*, and *Sex Toy Tales*. She is the editor of the series *Naughty Stories from A to Z* (Pretty Things Press) and *Best Bondage Erotica* (Cleis).

Sage Vivant ("Multiple Nudity") operates Custom Erotica Source (www.customeroticasource.com) and her work appears in *Best Women's Erotica*, *Mammoth Book of Best New Erotica*, *Naughty Stories II* and *III*, *Wicked Words 9*, and many other anthologies. She is the author of "29 Ways to Write Great Erotica" (www.29eroticways.com) and the editor of *Swing! Swapping, Swinging and Other Sinful Stories*. She teaches a class called *Writing for Your Sex Life* with author M. Christian in San Francisco.

Saskia Walker ("Skin on Skin") is British and lives with her partner, Mark, near the beautiful windswept landscape of the Yorkshire Moors. Saskia has travelled widely and believes that living in exotic countries contributed to her desire to write, that and an extremely active imagination! Creative writing has always been an important part of her life but has increasingly lured her away from all manner of bizarre careers to spend more time writing fiction. She has a BA in Art History, a Masters in Literature and writes across several genres. Visitors are welcome at: www.saskiawalker.co.uk

Mark Williams ("Tattoo You") is a forty-something married Chicagoan who is versatile, if nothing else. He has written everything from promotional material for Trump Plaza in Atlantic City to sketches for the WGN-TV children's program "The Bozo Show." He's been a correspondent/researcher for Playboy Magazine for many years, and is a polished professional stand-up comedian, as well. His short stories have appeared in *Best Bondage Erotica* (Cleis), *Down & Dirty* (PTP), and *Naughty Stories from A to Z, vol. 2 & 3* (PTP).

*"Clothes make the man. Naked people have little
or no influence in society."*
—Mark Twain

Naked Resources

Books:

Naked by David Sedaris
The Naked Chef by Jamie Oliver
The Naked Chef Takes Off by Jamie Oliver
Naked Happy Girls photographs by Andrew Einhorn
Naked Lunch by William S. Burroughs
Naked Pictures of Famous People by John Stewart

Movies:

The Naked Jungle
The Naked Prey

Music:

Blind Leading the Naked — Violent Femmes
Dance Naked — John Cougar Mellencamp
Let It Be...Naked — The Beatles
Naked — Talking Heads
Naked Baby Photos — Ben Folds
The Naked Ride Home — Jackson Browne
Naked Songs: Live — Rickie Lee Jones

Beauty Products:

Fresh "Naked Truth" Eye Shadow
Sebastian "Stark Naked" Shampoo
Sephora "Nearly Naked" Super Shimmer Lip Gloss
She She Cosmetics "Stark Naked" Barely There Lip Gloss
Sugar Shine "Naked" Lip Gloss
Trusunshine "Scrub and Go Naked"
Urban Decay "Naked" Ink
Urban Decay "Naked" Pleather Pencil
Vincent Longo "Naked" Lip Pencil

Pretty Things Press, Inc.

Naughty Stories
From A to Z

Naughty Stories
From A to Z—Volume 2

Naughty Stories
From A to Z—Volume 3

Bondage on
a Budget

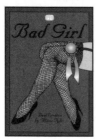

Bad Girl

30 Erotic Tales
Written Just For Him

30 Erotic Tales
Written Just For Her

Down and Dirty

Juicy Erotica

Naked Erotica

www.prettythingspress.com